The Day The Earth Stopped

By

Terry Godfrey

Technology can be our best friend, and technology can also be the biggest party pooper of our lives. It interrupts our own story, interrupts our ability to have a thought or a daydream, to imagine something wonderful, because we're too busy bridging the walk from the cafeteria back to the office on the cell phone.

Steven Spielberg

Information technology and business are becoming inextricably interwoven. I don't think anybody can talk meaningfully about one without the talking about the other.

Bill Gates

Tomorgen

Old English for **Tomorrow**

The Day The Earth Stopped

On board the ship Alpha, an eight-person crew, in route to Mars, 225 days from Earth. Much discussion had gone into the makeup of the Mars team. The professional and physical requirements were the deciding factors though.

The captain Mark White, past shuttle crew, now working with SCAMI a private corporation, intent on colonization of Mars. Second mate Janice White, Mark's wife and a prominent engineer-inventor. Mission doctor Emily Prater, equally capable in clinic surgery, or chemistry lab. Emily's husband, Richard Prater, mission botanist, and agronomist. Communications expert and electronics specialist Jacob Wells who is also a technology specialist. Lea Marten, the crew's geologist, and also a chemist. Robert Scott is the crew, microbiologist, and physicist. Dan Freeman they call their handyman, he has an uncanny ability to fix or build anything with whatever is available. Dan is also security specialist, and computer programmer, hacker.

Twenty-five days before, a supply ship landed on Mars at Colombia Hills in Gusev Crater. Today an automated supply ship is landing within a few kilometers of the first. On board the Alpha all hands are eagerly monitoring the landing, as is everyone in mission control back on Earth. Supply ship number three was only five days behind them, and would land right after they did.

The mars lander separates from the orbiter and begins it's decent. The orbiter is not to be wasted, on board is communications and observational equipment. It as the previous platform are to be the communications, and GPS satellites for Mars. With this equipment up to date photos of the first lander proves it is in exact position. Moments later an exited Alpha crew watch as lander 2 slowly settles to its resting place not fifty meters from the first lander. Now everything they need for their stay of one year and seven months is in position. Their mission is to prepare the site for colonization.

On the long-range plan, assembly of an orbital base to be used for future missions to the asteroid belt. Previous probes had proved the moons around Mars and the asteroids as very valuable mining prospects. SCAMI Space Colonization and Mining Ink, needed those resources to compensate for the expense's it had already invested.

The first things the crew had to attend to after landing would be to set up temporary habitat. Everything they should need and even or might need was on the two supply landers, other than natural resources.   The landing site had been chosen because water had been detected just below the surface. Water was needed not only for drinking, but converters needed large amounts for oxygen to breath, and hydrogen, for fuel. Though they could launch a return trip to

Earth at any time the optimal would be 1.6 years from landing.

There were enough supplies for two years, scheduling called for more supplies in a year and six months. The team hoped to have Mars base self-sustaining at some point, but for now it was conjecture as to wither this would be possible. Part of their problems to solve was building a permanent habitat, oxygen generator, and energy source.

...

In western Kansas Jason was starting another day of work. A few months earlier he had been promoted to area lineman for the County Electric Cooperative. He had taken over for Jack whom had retired after 45 years. Jack didn't trust computers, or high technology. Jason on the other hand, grew up with technology, and depended on its ability to assist in everyday functions.

Over the last few years automated, and remote-controlled switches had been installed all over the grid. Switches that can be operated from the dispatch office or even from computer console in the lineman's truck. Smart meters were installed at every consumer, whether household or commercial. These meters can be used to turn an account on, or off. To check usage, and get fundamental readings. Voltage regulators, and substation transformers, all digitally operated.

Communication with these devices is vital to the operation of any electric service provider in today's world. For some communication was microwave, others radio wave, and some a signal sent down the wire itself. Most equipment if communication was lost, was supposed to lock in the last position it was in. Failsafe though was to go to the open position.

Jack was glad to finally retire. The last few years had seen many high-tech advance's. He just did not trust the technology. His distrust wasn't totally unfounded either. The digital switches they had installed last year had lost communication several times, often as not, at 2 o'clock in the morning. Loosing communication, they would open and cause an outage over a large area.

Old time linemen were in touch with their neighbors and the consumers. Jack often had coffee with farmers and others he knew. Everyone depended on the line crews that kept the power going, and trusted these crews to work safely, and efficiently. With this new equipment outages seemed to be more frequent, but faster and easier to repair. The tolerance of the consumers for even the slightest power fluctuation was no longer reasonable though.

Jack now spent his days fishing, and enjoying life. He also raised a large garden from which he took fresh vegetables to the farmers market each week. A couple days a week he took his father to radiation treatments. On occasion he would travel across the state to visit with his son, and grandkids. Another favorite pastime was horseback riding.

Today Jason needed to check the repeaters in his area. A thunderstorm had gone through during the night and some of the repeaters were down. Communication to the meters would be lost till they were repaired. Each day the meters on prepaid needed to be checked online, if the account wasn't paid then they would be disconnected. This could not be done if communication with that particular meter was down. Often as not all he had to do was replace a fuse, but on occasion he would have to replace the control board. A digital board inside the control box mounted high enough on the pole that it took a bucket truck to reach it. These repeaters were placed strategically around the grid at locations the signal needed strengthened.

At one time there had been some concern to terrorist attacks on the power grids, but due to the large number of strategic points strung over such a large area, this was deemed unlikely. Even a large outage caused be one or two pieces of equipment failure or destruction could be rerouted or repaired in a short enough time. To cause truly catastrophic damage or power failure would take the loss of hundreds of devices spread over as many miles. A small group would be hard pressed to cause a perceptible effect before being found or the damage being restored. Todays linemen were just that efficient.

As Jason pulls his truck up next to the pole with the repeater mounted on it, he receives additional service orders on his computer. Connecting to the repeaters control via Wi-Fi and his laptop Jason diagnoses the problem, and preforms needed repairs. He calls his supervisor on his cell phone and waits while the signal strength is tested on that line segment. District line work now consisted of digital equipment maintenance as much as line work. He remembered stories Jack told him of early days on the line. A lineman would climb one pole after another all day long. Climb trees to trim them back from the line.

...

In NASA control center Houston Texas, Dr. Raymond Talbert was at his desk checking rosters and assignments for his personnel. Dr. Talbert as head of heliophysics research was in charge of a large team studying all things within our solar system. Most significant at the time is solar research. The Parker solar probe would soon be making another even closer loop around the sun. The data already collected was expected to be miniscule compared to what was to come. After each pass the information which was returned was more than triple the previous loop.

The Parker solar probe would loop around the sun then out to Venus loop around and return around the sun. Each time around the sun it would pass even closer than the trip before. The gas samples it was supposed to scoop up this trip and analyze could explain many things about solar flares and eruptions. The main fear of the mission was if the probe would be able to continually handle all the radiation, heat, and extreme elements that the sun was dishing out. On the last loop around the sun information was somewhat garbled, and distorted. Even now there were skips within the communication stream.

Dr. Talbert had three teams taking turns working around the clock to monitor all data and communication from the Parker probe. He had giving strict instructions that if anything out of the ordinary, or unexpected happened he was to be notified immediately. For now, he was on his way to watch his daughter play softball. Alisia Talbert was in high school with a 4.0 GPA, and an excellent fastpitch softball pitcher. Dr. Talbert had graduated from Princeton University, received his doctorate from MIT, and started research at the University of California, before being hired by NASA.

...

Along a small lake in a remote mountain in western Wyoming, Craig Taylor pulled in nice trout. Putting aside his fishing rod he strode back to his cave to cook dinner. Having tired of the hassle of modern day life Craig had sold everything and hid out in these mountains. Isolated as much as possible Craig lived totally off the grid. With no electronics of any sort, no electricity, and no communication, he was completely cut off from the rest of the world. Each day was filled with fishing, hunting or growing a few vegetables. In season he could find mushrooms, and assorted wild berries. A short trip down the mountain along the creek he could find wild onions.

For five years he lived here in a small cave he had found near the lake. Just inside there was a vent hole, and he was able to build a fire as the smoke was vented out the hole. The only time anyone came near was one year a couple deer hunters had been a mile away. They never knew that he was anywhere around.

Though he had brought an old henry rifle and a case of ammo, most of his hunting he used a bow and arrows. At times Craig would pan a little gold, but found very little color. Not that interested in gold he mostly tried panning for a distraction. Craig seldom wore city clothing, he saved them for his annual trip to town. He had buckskins, fur coats he had made from the hides of game. Tall and lean, with a beard down to his chest he looked like he belonged on a Duck Dynasty rerun. Although he looked, and lived like a hermit, Craig was educated and fairly intelligent. He had brought some pipe up the mountain, and tied them to a small pond upstream from his cave. Thus, he had running water in the cave, which flowed out and ran into the lake. The shallow stream where it flowed down to the lake was rock and he used it as his path. The running water washed away any tracks leaving no trail to his home.

Craig could hang meat in the vent and with a fire below burning green wood he could smoke meat to last a few weeks. After a few failures he was able to make some very good jerky. This did take a lot of time to make and required the use of salt. About an hour hike up the mountain the snow never melted. Here he would take some food and bury in airtight containers. The containers were so that animals wouldn't find his cache and steal it from him. Here he put away some meat and vegetables, for winter.

Some staples he couldn't find or make himself, such as salt, pepper, coffee, and sugar. He didn't have to have the sugar but he did miss coffee. One of the items he had brought with him was a large, comfortable backpack. Once a year Craig would hike down the mountain to a small-town, Dubois Wyoming. It was a three-day hike through some rough country. He would shed his buckskins and put on his city cloths before he reached the first signs of civilization. In town he would purchase the needed supplies, have one beer, get a newspaper, and a paperback novel. Well before dark he would be on his way back up the mountain.

Once on his way into town the local sheriff Gary had stopped to check him out. Showing his ID he told the sheriff he was just there to buy supplies. The sheriff did a search and found no record. As he was leaving the sheriff asked him if he needed a lift, and where he was going. Craig told him he had just got fed up with civilization and was living up in the mountains alone. The sheriff told him "well ok then, and if you ever need anything just get word to me".

Back in his cave after his annual trip Craig would read the newspaper over and over till it fell apart. He would read the novel over and over for a year till he had it memorized. The coffee and salt he would ration to last a year. He kept his money hid, but he marveled at how much prices rose each year. Still he figured he had enough money put back to outlast him, as his needs where few.

He didn't have anyone to worry about and no one to worry about him. This wasn't always true. Once he had been married, and had a child. They had both been killed by a drug addict looking for a little change to pay for his next fix. After a few years Craig had given up on justice, and the declining attitudes of the modern-day business society. Feeling more and more depressed, he just left. Now he had no one making demands on him, and he actually felt that he was in his element.

...

In O'Hare international airport, Captain John Colson was preparing to board his plane. Today he would be flying from here to LAX. Then later to DFW. He would have a long lay over in Dallas before being assigned his next flight schedule. He was a 747 pilot and todays airframe were one of the newer models. For some time now, he had been training and hoping to advance to one of the brand new 787's. John still liked the old 747 in which the pilot had more control flying.

John Colson had learned to fly in the Air Force as a bomber pilot. He was as of yet, in the Air Force Reserves. A Captain with the airline, he was a Colonel in the Reserves. On his time in the Reserve's he would fly simulated bombing missions over Nevada or Oklahoma. With the airline he would spend one night in Chicago, or maybe Las Angles, or Dallas, then maybe New York City. Among the airline flight crews John was considered one of if not the best fly by the pants pilot, and the most professional.

When he transfers to a 787 he would also be going to International flights. One plane one flight then a layover. Then another flight another airplane another city, and a layover. The ultimate way to see the world. The definitive ruin for a relationship. Already this job and lifestyle had cost him his family. Divorce had come two years ago while he was on the opposite coast. He did get to spend time with his kids, mostly online with facetime. They say, that he does pop in to see them more now though, but that may change with his new assignment. They live in Boston and he will be flying internationally, with less time in the states than abroad.

...

Bud Price was in the barn. The barn was actually a complete shop, where he built and refurbished old cars. Right now, he was putting the finishing touches on a ford model T truck. Hand cutting, staining and placing each board in the bed of the truck. Every detail pain's takingly accurate to the original design. The batteries he kept locked in an old unused refrigerator.

Though he did have a modern truck for everyday use around the farm, Bud enjoyed restoring the vintage vehicles. He always had one available for the local parade. In keeping with the vintage theme, he had his own gasoline tank mounted on a stand with free-flowing hose and valve.

Together with his wife of fifty-two years, they lived on the farm his grandad had homesteaded.

Donna his wife canned and put up vegetables, fruits and jams, on an old gas stove. This summer she had help lifting the old pressure cooker. Their granddaughters had been there to learn how to preserve food. What slowly was becoming a dying art. Though the girls said they were having a good time they would run off with their smart phones every chance they could.

The girls Penney 13 and Peggy 11 were from the big city. A smart phone was always in their hands. If asked a question, a few touches on the smart phone and they had an answer. Once Bud asked Penney where the name of her school came from, after a couple seconds typing on her smart phone she answered, "The first US President." Technology a great thing but sometimes we need to lay it aside and think for ourselves.

On his back-porch Bud had a smoker which he used to smoke meat and make homemade deer, and beef jerky. He had a large vegetable garden, several fruit trees. Each fall he hunted deer, and turkey. They raised several cattle, and when he was younger he had butchered beef, and hogs with his father.

...

New York City, Tom Backster is walking down the street, blue tooth in ear talking on phone while looking at stock market on an iPad. Not a minute of any day could go by without Tom tied to his phone and or iPad. Tom spent more time in front of a computer with 3 screens, than he did with anything else.

The only vacation he had taken he spent the entire time on his phone and iPad. The next dollar, and staying constantly in touch with his clients, was everything for Tom. He had never been able to have a relationship, because he was always to busy. The more technology advanced the busy it kept Tom. The less time he had for anyone else or personal time. What was personal time anyway, but a lost chance to earn some more money.

He lived in a small apartment which was fine because he spent very little time there. When at home he seldom watched tv or read a book instead he was busy on the computer or phone. Even though there was a kitchen in his apartment he had never fixed a meal there. His meals were at a vendor on the street or a restaurant with a client. He had plenty of money in his account, but no idea how to enjoy it.

...

Dallas Texas, Nathan Garret was on patrol. Eleven years as a police officer for Dallas PD Nathan was well aware of his neighborhood. Although younger, Nathan idolized the old-style cop on a beat. He would stop and talk to the merchants, and he would go to the park and walk through and visit with the people there. Sometimes he would be told of something that looked out of place, or suspicious. He would always check it out, and occasionally it would lead to an arrest.

Nathan had a radio link in one ear, with a blue tooth to his phone. In the car was a computer which tied him to all the information available at the station, or even worldwide. At the touch of a finger he could pull up any known information on anybody he could identify, or sometimes even photograph. On the job he was totally immersed in the work. When he signed off for the day, he went home, and by the time he had the uniform off, he was a family man and off the job.

His wife of six years Bethany, and four-year-old son Reed had his full attention. Bethany was a school teacher, and loved teaching young kids. Together they had a small house in the suburbs, a dog in the back yard, and a church a few blocks away. Bethany instead of using a blackboard used a smartboard. A video projector hung from the ceiling, and computer stations along one wall. Students where no longer kept from using their phones, instead they were encouraged to look up, or research with them.

Fixing dinner Bethany used the last egg, the smart refrigerator recorded and added it to her shopping list. Before walking into the living room to watch television, Nathan turned the lights and tv set on with voice activation. Before either had arrived home, the climate control had reset from away to home temperature. Although not an actual smart home, technological advances were enhancing their lives.

...

    Captain John Colson had landed his airplane in LAX. The passengers had all unloaded and new load of passengers were boarding for DFW. Soon he would be on his way to Dallas. The flight here had been uneventful, and so should the flight to DFW. Midweek flights usually held mostly seasoned business travelers. Once they would mix with the passengers, but not in several years. Now the flight crew stayed locked in the cockpit till on the ground, and stopped at the terminal. The flight attendants though had to deal with the passengers, and saw more than what the average person would believe.

    The passengers were supposed to watch the safety demonstrations at the beginning of the flight, but no one did. Still flying was the safest mode of travel, although never boring. Every week a flight attendant reports some idiots trying to join the mile-high club in the restroom. Practically daily someone would show up intoxicated. The seasoned business travelers have learned to ignore these, as well as the occasional baby crying.

CHAPTER 2

Dr. Talbert had just kissed his daughter on the check, as he put her to bed, then his cell phone rang. The shift supervisor asked that he return to the control center immediately. On the way out of the door, his wife hands him an overnight bag. Ray as his friends and family called him, open the garage door, started to unplug his electric car. He then looked at his 1967 panhead Harley Davidson, and decided to drive it this night.

As he pulled up to the gate the guard on duty looked closer than usual at his ID before saying "hey doc you really ought to wear a helmet when you ride that old hog". He had to show his badge again, press his palm against a palm reader before entering the main building. By now he had noticed the unusual activity for this late at night. On entering the control room, he was immediately briefed on the situation.

The Parker Solar Probe was off track, and communication with it was very erratic. Every means available was being used to determine its new trajectory, and to reestablish control. As the tracking information started coming in, it was soon concluded that the probe was on a collision course with the sun. Just how soon it would burn up they were unsure of. It had been designed to come closer to the sun each revolution, before swinging out around Venus. As it circled around Venus it had the chance to dissipate most of the heat it had picked up near the sun.

This was to be its fifth revolution. The plan was for the probe to make at least seven revolution each a little closer to the sun, before it burnt up or shot out into deep space like a rock from a sling. Now it was speeding even faster than the original design had allowed for, and gaining more speed every minute. The Parker Solar Probe was locked into the suns massive gravity well. Every conceivable effort was made to regain control, and divert it back onto course.

An hour went by without even a whisper from the probe, or any indication that it received any from the control center. After another hour with no contact all expectation of renewed control was lost. Dr Talbert curled up on the sofa in his office and tried to get a little rest. After dozing a short time, he was awakened with noise of hustling around in the control room. Washing his face and straightening his suit Dr Talbert walked into the control room.

The largest explosion ever recorded, or even dreamt of had just occurred on the sun. The death of Parker Solar Probe had been spectacular. Analyses showed the suns reaction to the intrusion into its realm as overwhelmingly extreme. The probe had been traveling at speeds much greater than any man-made object had ever traveled. The shear velocity had caused an explosion which left what now looked like a giant crater in the sun.

A crater which soon expanded into the largest dark spot ever heard of. Watching the event unfold Dr Talbert became very concerned. He called Washington and advised of an immediate solar flare, or event emergency. Within minutes all agencies on the list where notified. Satellites in orbit were powered down in hope of protecting their digital hardware. A message was sent to Alpha, though it was very unlikely they would be affected.

Confirming Dr Talbert's fear, a giant flare formed and grew till it looked as if it would literally lap out to the earth. Breaking loose it swirled, and streamed directly towards the earth. Calling Washington again Dr Talbert, recommended an even higher risk of danger from the imitate flare. An update was sent to Alpha. A decade old plan was activated. Shut down what could, backup as much software as possible, and shield everything in sight.

...

Tomorgen; old English for tomorrow, only tomorrow is now today. The first indications of what was to come was the loss of the closest satellites to the sun. They didn't just go dead they exploded. On the noon side of the earth people out of doors noticed an extremely bright and hot sun. Electronics and all digital circuits on the remaining satellites were fried. Minutes later these satellites either blew up, went soaring out of orbit, or came crashing down to earth. The International Space Station lost all power, the personnel on board at the time began experiencing extreme heat and radiation. Minutes later a fiery ball exploded on the outward side. The doomed station began its fatal decent to earth. On the day side of the world every cloud faded away. Temperatures soared, airplanes in the highest altitudes exploded in midflight.

Those aircraft that didn't blow up lost all power. Plastic circuit boards melted down. All but the oldest planes lost all control. As the wave hit the ground all power shut down without even a blink. All phones and radios went dead. Cars on the road shut off. People with pacemakers grabbed their chests and fell dead. In many locations people exposed to the sun burnt to death. Everything digital or electronic flashed and melted down. Thin plastic melted. Batteries exploded.

The first wave to hit the earth lasted over thirty hours, and was the strongest EMP ever imagined. A strong micro wave blanketed across the planet. Mini patches of plasma splattered across the planet, as if paint thrown onto a canvas from a distance. Then came waves of radiation. Not one cloud was left in the sky anywhere in the world. Then came the inconceivable, brightly burning small balls from the sky that grew as they fell. Some of the smaller ones burnt themselves out before hitting the ground. Others burnt through skyscrapers, or made deep holes in the earth. Later these were identified as probably being antimatter which burnt up while contacting an equal amount of matter.

Over forty-six hours later the waves finally moved on. Behind the earth was blackened and dying. Electronic emissions which had spewed out from the earth were no more. Left now only the erratic noise of a satellite to near a solar body. Not one man made object was left in orbit. A remaining piece of the Hubble was imbedded in the Louvre. What was left of the International Space Station crashed into the south pacific. Then a darkness, and quite fell across the earth, as it had been a couple centuries before. The only light was from fires burning unimpeded.

...

On board a Los Angeles class submarine, in the Pacific Ocean Captain James Weaver was on his way to the galley. The intercom declared captain to the bridge action alert coming in. Taking time only to grab a cup of coffee, he rushed to the bridge. There he met the XO and communications officer. Confirm authentication. Yes, sir I confirm it is authentic. As, do I says the XO. Ok let me read it.

Dive Dive Dive Emergency Dive take us as deep as she will go. This says that a massive EMP is about to hit along with unknown amounts of radiation. We are to go deep and wait for forty-eight hours before coming up. That this is not a drill and that it isn't any form of belligerent attack. The Earth could be hit with what may be the worst solar storm in history. At maximum depth we will stream the wire antennae and try to monitor via satellite.

After reaching their maximum depth as many of the crew that could crowded around the communications room. I have comsubpac and reported us at depth. They said to remain in contact as long as possible, if we lose contact to wait the forty-eight hours then to cautiously approach surface, and try to make contact. If contact is not possible to test atmosphere and proceed to nearest US port and offer assistance, if needed. Our number one priority is to protect the US coasts.

Only a few minutes after that message came through all communication went dead. The radio operator told the captain that it went staticky, then just died. It almost sounds as if the satellites were destroyed. The captain told the crew they might as well get back to their duties, that for now they were on their own.

...

Onboard the Alpha ship in route to Mars, all eyes were on monitors and enhanced images of the Earth. Since they were speeding, at an angle away from the wave created by the solar flare, the effects on them should be less devastating. As a precaution the crew powered down all electronics, and shielded everything which they possibly could. The crew then put on their EVA suits to help protect them from radiation. What they saw defied imagination. A distortion or blurry wave which tapered off on the sides, followed by a glowing, burning red white yellow and blue mass extending nearly back to the sun. The Earth totally engulfed in this maelstrom. The shape was as an inverted pyramid, the base leading the way out. The very edge of this leading line is what would hit them.

Within minutes the weaken flank of the wave passed over the Alpha ship, and crew. Radiation levels rose slightly, then dissipated. Robert Scott had kept his watch on his arm as a test. This watch stopped the moment the wave passed over them. So too had every piece of electronics which hadn't been powered down and protected. After ten hours Mark the mission commander decided to power up one spare radio, to test wither the consequences of the wave had truly passed. With this radio working fine all other gear was powered up. Soon the crew was all busy trying to determine the total outcome of the flare.

As soon as the equipment had all been tested, Jacob began sending signals back to mission control on Earth. For hours he continued trying to reach every possible base with no avail. Between moments of sending a signal he listened intently for any type of electronic emission from Earth. This went on for five days with no indications of life from Earth. The most powerful camera on board was aimed of earth, the only thing they were able to tell was that neither the Hubble nor the Space Lab was any longer in orbit.

The Alpha and crew were now only four days from Mars, and five days from landing. Mark called for a meeting to decide on their options. First, they could continue with their mission and land. There was the possibility that the last supply ship would run into problems. Having no control over it they weren't able to shut down that ships electronics, during the solar flare. The other option was to return to Earth. The second option was wrought with problems. Not least of all Mars and they were now at the most distant aperture from Earth. This greater distance would add to fuel problems with returning immediately. This could be overcome by sling shot maneuver around Mars. If they were to return to Earth would there be anything they could do to help, or would there be anyone to help.

Mission commander Mark White asked a few questions to facilitate the discussion, knowing full well the final decision fell on him. Forty minutes later as the debate seemed to conclude, Mark made his determination. Mark gave orders that they would prepare for landing on Mars, and to begin immediate construction of what may very well be, their permanent home.

Before they were to leave the orbiter in the mars lander, Jacob Wells, and Dan Freeman fashioned monitors aimed at earth. They also devised remote access and controls which they would be able to use from mars. In this manner they would be able to have a better look, and perhaps communications with earth. Not knowing the situation on earth was worrying each of them. Was the eight of them the last of humanity? Hopefully not, and someday they would hear from earth.

By the time they needed to board the lander for descent, all that could be done on the orbiter had been completed. The last supply ship was still following five days behind, and the best they could tell it was satisfactory. They released from the orbital craft and slowly dropped toward mars. At the precise altitude the engines fired allowing for a controlled landing within inches of their planned mission perimeters. Once landed and shut down each member of the crew began work setting up a temporary habitat.

Five days later construction of a permanent dwelling was well on the way. A temporary control center had been set up in the lander. Today was the day the last supply ship was to land. The location for landing was to be two kilometers from them. Even so everyone was in the lander, and watching the progress. No one dared voice their concerns for the badly needed supplies. As there still had not been any world from Earth, this could be the last of any modern food and equipment they would have to help them survive.

As the supply ship was on its way down, it was apparent that it was in trouble. It was coming down to fast and much farther away than planned. The thrusters had fired to start its decent, but they must have fired seconds later than programed. Once visual contact was made they watched in horror as it descended without the landing thrusters. Seconds later they did fire, but was it too late to keep it from crashing. The last they saw was a dust cloud rising just over the low hills. Giving some hope, there was no explosion. Dan lined up the dust cloud with the lander then bounded off to the nearest hill at a ninety-degree angle to get a bearing from there. Returning to the lander he calculated the bearing to the supply ship, and that the distance was approximately six kilometers.

A few hours later Mark, Lea, and Dan was on their way to the lander. Travel was by Ant, their name for a battery-operated dune buggy. Ant had been unloaded off of supply one and assembled a day earlier. Finding the crash site wasn't too difficult, as wind had pushed the dust away stringing it as an arrow pointing to the supply ship. As they approached the hills, it was obvious that they would have to hike the last few meters to the crash site.

Though only eighty meters from the ant the topography was very rough. What they found was the supply ship on its side. The landing struts had collapsed on contact with rocks where it fell. The side of the ship had ripped open spewing the precious cargo. Mark, Dan, and Lea began picking up and loading everything they could. It would take many trips back and forth to save as much as they could from the wreck. One of the larger crates which Mark had dug for, was a top of the line 3D printer.

The Mars Community as they were calling themselves, settled into the day to day work of survival. Richard, along with Lea's help built a green house, and started planting an assortment of crops. These plants not only would provide food, but would help with carbon dioxide, and provide some of their oxygen. Dan had dug a couple meters to mine for ice. Water from this ice was crucial for their survival. They had equipment to convert water to hydrogen and oxygen, but they would need large quantities of the ice. Also needing water would be the crops in the green house's. Another of their needs would be power, for this they had multiple sources. A backup generator which could run off the hydrogen, was set up and in use. Also, solar panels had been set up and in use. In storage and to be assembled were two wind generators. The use of these was an uncertainty, since to little facts was known of Martian wind.

Part of the habitat being constructed was laboratories, a control and communications center, and medical facility. Emily, Richard, and Jacob labored to complete the erection, and stocking of this important facility. Jacob continued monitoring for any possible transmission from earth to no avail. Each time he entered the communications room he would play back recordings eagerly listening for a possible artificial transmission. They had no indication as to the situation back on earth.

...

Over eastern Idaho nearly half way on his flight from Seattle to Chicago Captain John Colson was happy to be flying one of the older 747s for the last time. His next flight would be in a newer 787, or so he thought. With no warning but a few sparks and smoke all instruments went dead.

The engines whined to a stop. It took both pilot and copilot to wrestle with the flight controls. Not only was all instruments dead, so too were the radio, and intercom.

John asked the engineer to unlock the cabin door, and bring Debra the head flight attendant in. As the engineer sat back down and went back to work, John asked Debra to see to it that everyone was buckled in and start preparations for a possible crash landing. With no power to the controls maneuvering was extremely difficult. Keeping as level as possible they slowly bled altitude, and maintained a speed just above a stall.

There not being any runway near that they could possibly maneuver to, John was scanning the horizon for any location that he might have a chance of landing. Heavy forest and rough mountains were all he could see though. Getting lower and closer to the mountains, he was becoming desperate for even a level spot to come down on. At what was nearly the last moment he saw a fairly if short snowy plateau. Straining hard, and praying there were no hidden rocks John told everyone to brace for impact.

They touched down on the very edge of the snow field. Within a few yards the left wing seared off, and the rightwing slide along the ice and snow. The rightwing kept them upright and from sliding off the mountain. Feet from the far edge of the snow field they came to a rest. All the cabin crew was uninjured. Not knowing what had caused the total loss of power and communications John had little hope that anyone knew where they were, or even that they had crashed. Going through the plane he found that the left wing tearing off had also tore open the fuselage. Though several were dead and injured, there were over 250 survivors.

The engineer asked some volunteers to help open the luggage compartment and find warm clothing for as many as they could. Also, they checked every cell phone, and laptop, for possible communication. Not one piece of electronics would work though. Lost high on a mountain in freezing conditions with darkness coming on, they had little hope. Gathering what they could find that would burn, they built a fire to try and stay warm. How many could survive the night, would anybody be able to find them, or could they climb off the mountain, all unknown.

...

Up on the mountain which Craig lived there was little indication of what was happening. Craig had no cell phone, not even a watch. He was used to an occasional tremor from small earth quakes, but what he felt today was different. Craig thought that it felt like a shiver. As if the earth trembled from something very frightening. Minutes later he heard a sonic boom. Looking up he could see a fireball falling from the sky. Over the next few hours he observed many such fireballs.

As he was watching the sky he noticed an airliner coming down. It was totally quite as though all engines were out. The plane came lower and crashed onto the ice and snow higher up on the mountain. Grabbing his backpack, some rope, and a hatchet, he started up the mountain. Craig had little belief that he would find any survivors, but was determined to help if needed. The sun which looked very odd and bright set before he had even made the snow line. Looking back down the mountain he had a good view. Where he would normally see towns, light up for the night the only lights he could see was a few fires.

...

Jason was nearing the end of his day, and all seemed normal. On the way home the screen to his computer went blank. Then he noticed the cell phone in his pocket was getting warm. He pulled over to the side of the road as his diesel engine died. A light wisp of smoke came from his cell phone and it too was dead. As a last-ditch effort, he picked up the radio to call dispatch, but no luck with it. Fifteen miles from home and twenty miles from the office not another car in sight, Jason had no idea what was happening nor what to do next.

Finally giving up on restarting the motor, or of getting anywhere with any of his electronic devises, Jason started walking down the road. Remembering a repeater was about a mile up line he planned on unplugging it and perhaps drawing the attention of dispatch.

Back at the County Electric Cooperative, dispatch was just becoming aware of disaster. They were well adapted, to disaster. From ice storm, to tornado, to an occasional flood they had weathered many disasters. The lead dispatcher, Mike had worked through many such events. Call in the director, supervisors, all crews and support personnel. This time there was no indications of how much line was off. All screens, computers, radio, and phones were dead. Even though they had a large backup generator to power the facility there was no power. First, he went out to the generator and tried to start it. Unable to get it to even turn over, he noticed Karen in the parking lot trying to start her car. It was soon determined that nothing would work or run.

Frustration was driving everyone to crowd into dispatch. Donnie the director soon organized everyone towards tasks aimed at getting power back on. They needed to find working transportation, and communication. The mechanic came in from the parking lot to advise them that none of the cars or trucks would run, all of the electronic ignitions were fused. The techs had said much the same about all cell phones radios, and computers. Scent candles that had been rounded up from different desk were used to light up the dispatch and meeting room. Donnie shared the memo that he had received the day before, about an eminent solar flare. They had seen many of these in the past with little problems.

When morning arrived, a runner was sent to the phone company's office to find out it any chance of any communication would be available. The phone company had no idea it or when they would ever be able to reestablish cell or data communication. Although they were sure if power was restored to their switch house's that hardwired phones could be back in use soon. The runner relayed the information back to Donnie.

A couple old diesel generators that had been in storage for many years had been pulled out by the mechanic. He had the idea that not having electronic ignition if they could be cleaned and fuel they might be used to provide emergency power. These generators had been put aside years ago as being inefficient, and undersized. Being very heavy it took all the man power they could muster to load one on a small trailer. They then had to push the trailer by hand to the phone companies switch house, two miles away. The other generator, they used to power up their own dispatch office.

Even though they now had power to the dispatch, none of the electronic equipment would work. Although the old phone line did now work. Communication with the generation and transmission company was reestablished. There was some power available on the grid but at only a small percentage of peak efficiency. The up side was that very little was in use at this time. The executives of the cooperative were just getting a handle of the scope of the disaster. They were fairly certain that an extremely devastating solar flare had caused a massive EMP burst which had fried all electronics wither or not it had been powered up.

Jason had no luck at the repeater. He continued walking till he got to his house. With no power and still no way to communicate, he kept on walking till he arrived at the office. Here he found that most of the employees had come in. Electric company employees have always been very dedicated to their work.

A farmer from three miles outside of town rode up to the cooperatives parking lot on a horse. He was only a little concerned about when he might get electricity back on, but he offered any help he could provide. A few hours later he returned with five horses and saddles. These were tied behind a wagon and a pair of draft horses he used in parades. Leaving all but one saddle horse he rode back home, he laughed and said, "they could just take it off my next month's electric bill".

A rider was sent out to the nearest substation to see if he could tell the condition to that point. Finding the station transformer humming and all the automated switches open, he returned to the office to report. Donnie after receiving the report realized he only had one or two linemen which could operate manual testing, and switching, and with no remote communication, they needed old time linemen. He made what calls he could and sent out riders to find the most recently retired linemen.

Later they would have to bring in retired accountants, and billing clerks that knew how to keep books on paper, instead of on computer. After being depressed and feeling useless the technology personnel began trying to figure how to repair the computers. A day later the techs were even more depressed. All circuit boards and hard drives were fried. Thereby all information would be lost. The next day they built a simple circuit board from scratch, doing so they discovered that any new electronics would work.

Now all they had to do was get all power restored, and replace all electronics. Then reprogram everything from scratch. A daunting task, but they now had a renewed hope. With a slight smile they entered Donnie's office to give him a report on what it would entail. Though it would take a couple of years they could get their part of the world back online and on track.

...

In NASA Mission control center Houston Texas, Dr. Talbert watched as all consoles either went dead or some sparked and flashed. Within minutes every means he used to monitor the solar system was off, as was even the lights and air. Sometime later maintenance informed them that nothing could be done for now. Only after power was restored and all components replaced could they possibly monitor any systems left. Dr Talbert decided he might as well go home. He told everyone to get a good night sleep, and to be thinking of ways to check on and open communications with the Alpha crew.

In the parking lot everyone discovered they were going to have to walk to get anywhere. Dr. Talbert looking at his vintage Harley smiled as he kicked it to life. He could feel the hard stares as he roared towards to gate, and guard house. The guard at the gate said, "Doc, you would have the only thing left running on the planet wouldn't you. Grinning Dr Talbert waved as he drove off towards his home.

CHAPTER 3

Nathan was at home watching tv when it went off, since the lights also went off he assumed the power was off. He picked up his cell phone to call the power company, only to find it dead too. Thinking this odd he picked up his iPad planning on using the power companies ap to report the outage, this too was dead. At that time, he heard an explosion some distance away. Stepping outside he could see smoke rising from DFW airport, or very near there.

Now very concerned Nathan went to his patrol car, and found it would not start nor could he get anything from the radio. He then tried his personal car, nothing seemed to work. Knowing if this was very wide spread they would need all the officers to come in. Kissing his wife good bye, and telling her to stay home, he dressed in his uniform and rode his bicycle to the office.

Once at the office he and some others with bicycles were given the more distant areas to patrol. Their orders were to maintain order as much as possible. They were reminded that the job was to protect and serve. The public will be very scared, and full of question. They weren't the only ones. Few if any had a notion of what was happening. Stressed people would be thirsty. Nathan asked for as many bottles of water as he could carry in his back pack.

On the street Nathan didn't rush to his patrol area, instead he slowly pedaled his way, and stopped to talk with people on the street. As expected everyone wanted to know what was happening. His patrol area wasn't too far from his home. Each officer was assigned to an area as close as possible to their home as could be, or to the main office. They had been informed that land line phones would be the first communication to come back on, they were encouraged to find or connect old style ring phones at their homes. Telephones like that could work with only the power from the phone company. This they were not to tell the general public. Police, fire, ambulance, hospital, communication, and power companies had first priority for use of the phone lines.

One of the worst worries for the police was vandalism. In an attempt to inhibit this, they placed as many officers as they could on the streets. Investigators, and plain cloths officers were in uniform, and on the street.

Nathan was pedaling through a neighborhood not too far from home when a teenager ran out flagging him down. Entering the house with the teen he found the teens mother holding the father, which was having trouble breathing. Nathan made sure she knew how to administer CPR if needed, and told her he would get more help. He pedaled as fast as he could to the nearest fire station which also had an EMT crew. At the fire station he met with the EMT's which had a large running riding mower with a trailer attached. They proceeded to the address Nathan had given them.

Continuing on down the street, Nathan came across an elderly lady sitting on the curb. He stopped to check on her. She said she would be ok that she was just wore out. He gave her a bottle of water and she responded with a warm smile, and seemed a hundred percent better. She asked what had happened. Nathan told her he didn't know any more than she did at this time, but if everyone would work together and help each other, then they would all be ok. Smiling she nodded in agreement, as Nathan rode off.

He started down one of the business streets, dodging around stalled cars as he saw a confrontation in the front of a food chain. Dropping his bicycle, he hurried through the door with his hand near his gun. "What is going on here?" he asked. Two teens dropped the beer in their hands and ran out the door. "I didn't think they really wanted to become criminal" the store clerk proclaimed. The clerk told Nathan he knew the kid's families, and he thought he could talk to them. Nathan told him that would be fine, but If that didn't work, the next time he came by he would take their names and deal with them himself.

Midday Nathan rode into his driveway. He pulled out an old dial type telephone that was in his closet floor, and connected it to the phone line. Checking he did have a dial tone, so he called the office. He reported on all that had happened that day. He was told to try to get some sleep and call in just after sunset. They wanted as many officers on duty as they could get for night. Hopefully the sight of a police officer walking or riding by might deter some crime.

Nathan dozed off and on for a few hours. At dusk his wife had some food for him to eat. While eating some neighbors came by hoping he knew more about what was happening than they did. Nathan told them the same thing he had told the old lady. When he called in he did learn that it had been caused by the worst solar flare ever imagined. Also, that in a few days power might be restored to priority locations, then slowly across the network.

Although his legs where aching Nathan rode out to work on his bicycle. As he came into an intersection he noticed a small group coming towards him about a block away. Holding to the shadows he didn't think they had seen him. He saw one was pulling a small wagon and another was peering in windows. He knew they were looking for a place to loot. He also knew he had no way of calling for backup. Gritting his teeth, and saying a little prayer he stepped off his bike, and started advancing toward them in the shadows. Just before he stepped out in front of them he saw another figure following behind them. Waiting a second, and watching closer to the figure behind he was pleased to see it was another officer.

The guy peering into windows raised a brick as if he was going to break the window, so Nathan stepped out in front of them all, saying Dallas PD everyone freeze. One of them started mouthing off while reaching behind himself, saying your all alone. The officer behind them approached and said "no his not alone". Realizing that there was an officer in front and one behind them they said "ah we aren't doing anything." That is good then. You had all better split up right now, and go on home. Don't let me catch you out at night like this again.

In times of disaster most people come to together to help each other. There are those though that try to take advantage of the situation. Over all, kindness and self-sacrifice proved the worth of human nature. When people worked together for the better of all, then nothing can defeat them.

On the next street Nathan rode upon a man with a shotgun standing in the middle of the street. As he cautiously approached the man, he recognized him as one of the store owners. "Sir just what are you doing" Nathan asked. The store owner said we know you are all working hard as you can to protect us, but on this street, we are taking turns guarding our stores. Hopefully you won't have to use that shotgun. You should all carry a whistle. If you see, or hear anything then blow as hard and long as you can. We are out and around. An officer will be here as fast as they can.

...

Worldwide the damage and effects were similar, but in each city the response was different. Tom was at his desk on the computer with three screens working on a deal worth close to a million dollars. He hadn't even noticed the brightness of the sun through the windows of his corner office. He did notice when all the screens went off the computer died and all the lights went off. Thinking he would sue someone if this was another blackout he looked out the window to see an airplane falling from the sky. A chill ran down his back as he thought this might be another terrorist attack. Tom spent an hour trying every cell phone and computer available.

With no working electronics he had no idea what to do.

After a while he went into the hall and tried the elevators, which didn't work. Cussing his luck, he heard someone yelling from inside the elevator. They suggested he try to pry the door open so that they could get out. He poked his ink pen between the doors and tried prying them open, only the have the pen break in his hands. The voice inside the elevator, told him that there should be a fire axe in a box near the elevator doors. Hoping that they didn't know what he had tried he broke the glass and used the axe to pry the door open. Four people were in the elevator, and all seemed very glad to be out.

Now to get out of the building one hundred and sixteen stories up. Tom never in his life contemplated walking that many stairs. Even going down he wasn't sure it would be possible. He had slept in his office on more than one occasion, and had food for just such times. He also had plenty of alcohol to last. Rather than attempt such a long walk he decided he would wait out the storm. As night came on he had a perfect view to all around, and not one light shone anywhere. With no communications, no connection to the world wide web, the markets, or the news, Tom was not only bored but near frantic. He couldn't remember a time when he had been so unconnected. After five doubles he finally slept.

Awakening he was sure the power and computers would be back on, but no, they weren't. Yelling out there was no one to answer. He was the only person left on that floor. Six floors down someone else had spent the night in the building, but otherwise everyone had left. By noon he had decided that if by tomorrow morning the power wasn't back on he would climb down the stairs. He would start early in the morning so he would have all day to see going down. Looking out over the bay he saw the USS Constitution with all sails extended moving out past the Statue of Liberty.

Unknown to him the navy ship had orders to sail, and make personal contact with England and Europe, then return home. Other ships where sailing, but few high-tech navy. Only the very old analog ships would even run. The USS Constitution though a very old sailing vessel, was armed, and recognizable as a USA Naval ship, not only that she was faster than most cargo ships still running.

The next morning, he went down, it did take most of the day to get down. It was just over ten blocks to his apartment so he started going that way. He had thought he would be able to get a cab, but when he made it to the street he could see all vehicles were abandoned. On his way he noticed store fronts broken into and looting everywhere. This was not how it was supposed to be. Tom soon was wishing he had stayed in his office. By the time he had reached his apartment Tom had seen multiple gangs looting and molesting everything in sight. Only sheer luck and extreme fear had kept him from falling into troubles paws.

Locking himself into his apartment Tom was determined to stay there as long as he could. The next day that became obviously impossible. He soon realized he had very little food in his apartment. He would have to venture out within a couple of days. He watched out the window day and night to see what was happening. He had never associated with others unless it was business, so no one checked on him. On the second day he was without any food, and he had seen a street vendor out around noon. He went out to meet him. He found the vendor on the corner, but it cost him twenty dollars for two hot dogs. Taking his hot dogs back to his apartment Tom wasn't sure how this was going to play out. He only had a couple more twenties in cash on him. The vendor told him plastic wasn't good anymore.

The street vendor was one of few still operating in the big city. He had a propane cook stove mounted in his hand pushed cart. He had a store that knew him and would sell him buns and wieners day or night. Charging a little more than double right now seemed like only good business since. Anyway, the store was charging him more than normal. In the past he had often given left overs to the homeless at the end of the day, but not now. You eat you pay.

...

On the farm a few miles northwest of Dallas. Bud Price was feeding livestock. His granddaughters were on their cell phones texting friends when the phones went dead. Looking up the lights were off and the tv had went off. Running out to the barn screaming for grandpa the girls were mad that they were deprived of their online time. Somehow, they just knew he had shut them off. Checking around Bud soon figured out that nothing worked. Before walking into town or saddling up the old mare, he tried the model T truck. It started right up and ran fine.

Telling everyone to stay in the house he headed for town, to see what was going on. Puttering into town, people along the road stared at him with envy. In town he picked up a couple things they needed at home, including coffee, and went to the post office. There he was asked to wait till the police chief came. He was asked if he would be willing to drive back and forth to Fort Worth till regular communication was established. If not, would he allow them to use his truck.

He asked to take the supplies he had home then he would be happy to help out. They asked that he not reveal what he heard in the messages to others. It was explained that they didn't want to cause a panic. Bud said ok, but just how bad is it. What happened? He was told that the best anyone knew at that time was that a solar flare had knocked out all electronics. It might be a few years before everything was back to normal.

He was told that soon food would be hard to get, as every other commodity. That in the next few days some power might be restored and hard line telephone service could be available. Hearing that he advised them that he and most of the other farmers would have produce available, if they could get them to town.

On returning home Bud's granddaughters wanted to know just what was going to happen. He told them, they would be too busy helping out to notice the lack of cell phone usage. They would have to pick berries, and help can. Many people would be dependent on the food that they could provide. It would take the combined effort of all of them to produce all the food it would take to feed everyone.

The large corporate farms, where dependent on technology to operate. The small family farms, and the even smaller truck farms, could produce with no high tech. The more elbow grease, and or help the more they could produce. Getting it from here and there to market was the problem. In the past safety regulations prohibited them from selling openly to the public.

...

Riding his Harley through the gate Dr. Talbert was apprehensive about their chances of reestablishing communications with the Alpha crew. He also knew that if communication wasn't made they may never hear from that crew again. The wave that had hit the Earth would have been very devastating to a craft in space if it had hit them with the same strength if had hit the Earth. To many unknowns they must find a way to communicate with the team. They should be on Mars by now if all went well for them.

Carl and five of his best scientists, hadn't gone home. He had an idea and they worked through the night, on it. As lead communications specialist he felt responsibly for renewing contact with the Alpha crew. His great grandfather had been a communications specialist on old sailing ships, and used whale oil signal lamps. He had one such lamp sitting on his desk. Thinking of making contact he had looked right at the lamp, and the thought came to him. He wasn't the only one to work all night ether. The chief mechanic labored all night rebuilding a backup generator with a carburetor, rather than electronic ignition.

Once inside the building Dr Talbert called a meeting to discuss possible ways to reach them. Carl had a far-fetched idea, but it was the only idea. That was to use the brightest and tightest beamed light they could at the Mars base and signal with old Morse code. They would have to keep the best telescope available pinned to the area watching for a reply, and they would have to keep it manned at all times. As this was the only idea, Dr Talbert told them to get on it right away. He was to be notified immediately of any response, day or night. Before the day was over a signal was being sent out across the void of space, hoping for a response.

The signal was being sent out every 15 minutes, and two of the strongest telescopes were trained on the landing site and the planned location of the orbiter. The telescopes had personnel, watching around the clock. The signal would take 19 minutes to arrive at Mars and if a response were made, another 19 minutes for the return. Carl sent word to Dr Talbert they had started sending, and within five minutes the communications center was crowded with eagerly watching people.

...

In the communications booth in the Mars Colony habitat an alarm starting buzzing. Slowly awakening from the pulsating loud sound Jacob realized the cause. Without dressing he ran to the communications booth. Turning the alarm off he then started replaying the recording of the monitors of earth from the orbiter. Laughing boisterously, he started writing down a message from the command center. Setting off the emergency alarm to wake everyone else Jacob double checked the message. The entire Alpha crew came running in, and finding Jacob laughing they though he might have been playing a joke on them. Mark asked what was going on.

Five minutes ago, I received message from Earth. It simply states Alpha are you there, what is your situation. They are signaling with a light signal, and Morse code, not a radio. I can respond but, I will need help building and setting up equipment to send a light signal from here. We also need to decide what to say. It will need to be fairly short. After a brief discussion a return message was formulated.

The entire crew worked together for 4 hours to fabricate a light signal. A range finding laser was used, and connected to the communications computer. They all crowed into the communications booth as Jacob typed in the message to send back to Earth. As he finished by hitting the send key, Dan asked how long it would be till they might hear back. Checking on the computer it was determined that it would take around 40 to 45 minutes.

...

Just over five hours after they had begun sending a message to Mars, a technician watching the telescope facing the landing site on Mars yelled out "I see them." Having someone write down the dots and dashes, he watched the same message three times. Confirming it was one message, and they had it copied correctly they deciphered the code. Mission Control from Mars Colony great to hear from you. All is good here. What happened, and how are our families?

As much as was known was sent out to Mars, which was very little other than how and what had happened. Personal information and effects other than locally were unknown at the time. Dr Talbert informed them that hope was that they would have the ability to send and receive radio within the next few months. At which time hopefully, they could share more detailed data, and information. Just how much data would be left on Earth was still unknown, but the computers on Mars and aboard the orbiter had a wealth of information. At best it would probably be years before another launch to Mars would be possible. There would be no resupply ships, rescue, or replacement personnel. Colonist would be very unlikely for many years.

It was mutually decided that for now the Mars Colony would best continue on for one and a half years, then discuss options at that time. They could launch, and link up with the orbiter, then return to Earth. It would be a one-way trip though with little chance of anyone returning back to Mars for the foreseeable future. Another option would be for part of the crew to remain on Mars, and some to return to Earth. They had at least a year to decide.

The communications team continued to monitor for and send messages to Mars. The majority of Mission Control scientist, and technicians struggled to rebuild control and monitoring systems.   Some were brought back online sooner using antiquated analog equipment. Digital electronic had to all be built from scratch. In the next few months as, new computers were made available, books and files were brought out of storage. The information then had to be programed into the computers. Hours and hours of typing.

...

CHAPTER 4

Craig approached the crash site with little hope of finding anyone alive. The crash was high on Hard Luck Mountain near Red Tops. As he came within view of the airplane, he could see movement, and a small fire. Finding hundreds alive he started thinking of how to get them all down off the mountain. First, he knew he had to get them someplace warmer than here. Asking around as to who was in charge Craig met Captain John Colson. Craig told John about his cave, and that it was a three-day hike off the mountain.

Gathering up all the able-bodied men, they prepared to carry all the injured down to Craig's cave. Keeping everyone together they proceeded down to the cave. For the night all of the injured, children, and elderly stayed in the cave. A large fire was kept blazing to help keep them warm. Other large fires were lite to help keep everyone else warm. Craig help to prepare something for everybody to eat.

The next morning with directions from Craig the first officer stayed with the weak and injured at the cave. Craig, John and as many as could hike for three days started down the mountain. Talking amongst themselves, nobody knew for sure what had happened. All the flight crew knew for sure was that all equipment had went dark. The cell phones that had been tried didn't work. They weren't just out of range from any towers, they wouldn't even turn on.

Noon on the third day a motley looking group of seventy-four was straggling into town. A lady walking across the street spotted them, and went to the sheriff office to tell Gary. Rushing out to meet them he recognized Craig the mountain man in front leading them. It looked like there was an airline pilot with Craig, and a large number following.

After getting all the survivors, except for Captain John into homes, Gary sent out for all the local hunters, and anyone that could help on the mountain. All the horses and what all-terrain vehicles that would work was rounded up. They prepared an expedition to go back up the mountain and bring all the other survivors down. On the way up the mountain Craig showed Gary the easiest route to take. They used hatchets and axes to clear a path, to make the return trip easier for the injured. The more time he spent around Craig to more Gary liked and respected him. Traveling right up till dark each night They made it back to the cave late on the fifth night after the crash.

Though the last two trips up and down had been made in two and half days each, it would take them four days to get down this trip. Craig lead the expedition back down the mountain again. A young lady separated from everyone else and walked near Craig most of the time. Melinda was very pretty in a tom boyish way. She talked to Craig about how long he had lived on the mountain and how. The first two days either Gary or John had hung around near, kind of as an unofficial chaperone. Melinda finally opened up to Craig and told him she had nobody. Her mother had died years before and her father was one of the passengers whose seat went out the hole by the wing.

When they all came into the town, they found the towns folk ready for them. Places in homes had been prepared, and a makeshift hospital had been set up in the school gymnasium. Every person with any medical training was ready to help. Craig spent the night in town helping out. That night Melinda came to him asking if she could go back with him up the mountain. John having overheard walked over and asked how old she was. Melinda said "not that it matters, but I'm nineteen".

John told Craig that if he was thinking about taking her with him to meet with him, and sheriff Gary first thing in the morning over breakfast, with Melinda. Over breakfast they listened to Melinda tell how she thought, living off the grid would be her kind of life, and how over the last few days she had fell in love with Craig. Hearing her talk Craig realized he had been falling in love with her too, but had mentally avoided it, because she was a few years younger. Since she was of age and had no one, they agreed to help them get married before going back up the mountain.

They were married that day. Hand written and copied paper was filled with the signatures of the local preacher, and Gary. They made plans to spend one more night in town, gather all the supplies they could carry, and leave at dawn the next morning. A couple hours before sunset a noise was heard. Most everyone came rushing out onto the streets to see an army hummer coming into town.

Sgt. Baker, and private Nelson, asked to speak to the sheriff or mayor. Sheriff Gary came walked over to speak to them, while trying to quite everyone down enough that they could talk. The army had enough equipment EMP shielded, they had sent several out to contact surrounding towns. Sgt. Baker informed them that the trouble had been a solar event unlike anything ever experienced before, and that it should all be over. The bad news was that most all digital devices and electronics was destroyed. As far as anyone was able to tell all GPS, communication, and other satellites were destroyed.

Gary informed the army that they had two hundred and fifty survivors from an airliner that had come down in the mountains, including some that were injured. Sgt. Baker immediately called his base on a two-way radio. The military had working radio's that was designed to be used after a nuclear attack. All military in every branch were being used to help with civilian affairs. The base sent word that they would send a truck to evacuate the wounded to a working medical facility. The Sgt, and private were invited to spend the night in town. A community meal was prepared, and shared with them and with the survivors from the plane.

The next morning Gary walked with Craig and Melinda to the edge of town. "I would wish you well, but I have little doubt that the two of you will be just fine. You have been up there living without any modern devices for so long you're not dependent on anything that's gone. You two will probably be better off than any of us."

"We will still be coming down for supplies. If you need anything get word to me. I could bring some meat from time to time if needed. I'll have to stock back up before winter though, the survivors about cleaned me out in one night" said Craig. They also made plans to retrieve the personal effects off the plane later if the weather allowed. Craig asked that the sheriff not disclose to any more than needed the location of his cave. Gary sent a set of flares with Craig just in case Craig every needed help.

Craig and Melinda began the three day hike to her new home. Though a couple weeks ago anyone else would have said they had nothing, they felt as if they were very blessed. For them all they needed was each other, and what the mountain could provide them. With all the damage, and as many as had died, Craig felt sure they would be left alone, and he would have no more intrusions, into his hideout. A couple weeks later Gary showed up.

Gary had a team going to the crash site and needed Craig's help. He had left the team a few kilometers away, not to bring them to Craig and Melinda's home. Craig and Melinda went with Gary to lead them to the crash site. The team consisted of four LTATV's with six US army personnel. Craig, and Melinda climbed into one of the oversized ATV's with a sergeant. Their mission to retrieve the black boxes and certain personal items from the plane. Also, to take pictures and document as much as they could. As they were there Melinda found her luggage and was permitted to take it with her. Now she would have some of her own clothing to wear.

Gary told Craig, and Melinda that the power had come back on to the town but they were encouraged not to use any more than necessary to conserve as much as possible. The power was being restored, across the country, but generation capacity was still very low. The grid would not be able to handle high loads for some time. Craig said "well we won't be added any to the load at all, but glad to hear the rest of the world is starting to return to some normalcy."

As the army had all the LTATV's loaded fully, Craig and Melinda choose to walk home. Saying their goodbyes, Craig told Gary they would come down early in the spring. With winter about to sit in they needed to hunt some more and prepare to hole up for the winter. Gary told them so long and that he wished them the best.

Captain John Colson sat alone in a window of the sheriff's home. He wondered if his kids were ok. He no longer had any way to contact them, and had no idea how they, or his ex were. John knew he was not to blame for the crash nor that he would in any way be blamed for it, but he still felt bad for losing some lives. The survivors all called him a hero for getting them down, yet he wondered if he might have been able to save everyone.

The army personnel had told him that many airplanes had crash with no survivors. That in fact there were very few that had made it down with any alive. This was some consolation, but he still wished he could have got them all down ok. Also, on his mind was that he no longer would have a job, or anyway to provide for himself. All he really knew was flying, and that didn't look to be happening anytime soon.

On returning from the mountain the army team stopped in town. Gary got out and Sgt Baker came to him. They wanted him to go with them and he was to get to South Dakota as soon as possible to an US Air Force Base there. He would be flying again and very soon. Part of the US military strategy for nuclear attack was to have back up electronics in storage in a static free environment. How he would get to South Dakota he had no idea, but the military had that taken care of. They loaded onto trucks with the LTATV's, the army team and ten hours later was in Ft. Missoula Montana.

There Captain John was inducted and signed up for active duty. He then boarded a waiting UH1 helicopter for Ellsworth Air Force Base in South Dakota. The UH1 being an older analog helicopter for the most part was still operating.

...

Tom was again getting hungry in his apartment in New York City. It had been nearly a day since he had anything to eat. He hadn't seen the hot dog vendor nor any other that he might buy food from outside his window. He finally was about ready to venture out again. At times he had seen roaming thugs vandalizing the neighborhood. Tom started out his door, looking both ways he noticed another man coming out, a couple doors down and across the street. Then hearing a load yell, he looked farther down the street to see a gang of thugs coming their way. In horror he watched as they mugged and robbed his neighbor. He ran back into his apartment, locked and bolted all doors, and windows.

It was another twenty-four hours later before he, in desperation tried to exit again. This time he made it all the way to the corner market without seeing anything frightening. The market did have electricity. At the market he spent his last few dollars on what food he could find that might last. Nearly all canned meat and food had already been sold out. There was no bottled water or much other staples. Having been thirty some hours since he had eaten anything, he was thrilled with what he was able to purchase.

Tom returned home with what he hoped would last him a couple days. Once home he locked himself into a solitude which he had never known since the black out. Black out that is all he could think of which was causing this. Yet he thought of seeing the sail ships leaving the harbor. Something was drastically wrong, and someone would pay. He had never known of the television being off for this many days. He desperately needed to be back in touch; with his clients, and with the market. He could not make money setting home with no contact.

Staring out of his window he could see very few ships moving in the harbor. Nor did he see any vehicles moving on the street. Here and there he did see bicycles and push carts stirring. What few pedestrians he saw mostly traveled in small groups. Although he wasn't sure wither or not they might be belligerent. The unknown and fear kept him alone in his apartment, till hunger drove him out.

Three days later running out of food again, he had to leave his apartment. At the market they had more food, but he did not have cash to pay, and they could not accept his cards. He was told that three blocks over a bank had power and was open. Perhaps they could honor his credit. Shaking with fear he started towards the bank. Most stores he passed had broken glass and had been looted. If he spotted another on the street they usually ran.

When he got to the bank and entered, he was met at the door with two uniformed police officers. They asked him what he wanted. He told them he was out of food and cash, and had been told he needed cash to buy food. He just wanted to access some of his money. The officer checked him for any weapons and allowed him to approach the teller. At the teller he showed his identification, and his credit card. He then asked if he could get some cash money so he could buy food. As his account was with a recognized Institution, they issued the cash he needed.

Tom headed out the door and was stopped by the officers, again. They gave him a wad of paper and told him to throw it down and act furious as he exited the door. They then explained he might be watched, and if those watching thought he had been successful getting money, they would rob him. Walking out the door he threw the wad of paper on the sidewalk and kicked it cussing loudly. He then walked back to the market without any trouble. This time he was able to purchase some canned meat and a five-gallon bottle of water. Before he started home his neighbor which had been robbed a few days before came in. Tom waited till he was finished and together they went back to their street. For once in his life Tom had allied with someone else. He was fast learning he couldn't always depend on his own abilities and technology.

He had plenty of money in his account, but how long would he be able to access it and how long would he be able to find food to buy. Additionally, how many times would he be able to make the trip to the bank and market without meeting one of those gangs? He knew he needed to get to know his neighbors so that they could group together for these trips out. Not understanding the mentality behind the decision, the herd motivation was coming back into application.

...

After forty-eight hours Captain James Weaver ordered the boat brought up to periscope depth. Here they slowed to 5 knots, and raised the antennae. With no sounds at all coming in over the radio, he raised the periscope for a look around. Seeing nothing, nor hearing anything either on radio, radar, or sonar, he decided to come to the surface. Calling for action stations so that they could dive again in a hurry if needed they surfaced.

He ordered radio to try every frequency starting with military. The first men on deck were to test for radiation, anything to high, and they would submerge. They found no radiation, and no signal of any kind on the radio. The only sound on sonar was some whales singing.

Not making any contact and not getting any GPS coordinates, they took compass and sight readings. As it was close to night fall they stayed on the surface listening and taking test till dark. At dark they got star readings to pin point their exact location. As James figured there would be some others going to Hawaii, and they were as close to the Oregon coast he set coarse for Astoria, Oregon on the Columbia river.

They submerged the boat and cruised at a minimum depth continually listening and trying to make contact.   A few days later they surfaced again just off the coast of Oregon. They slowly cruised up the Columbia river at surface battle stations. As they approached the river they spotted a couple of sail boats moving. Steering up the river they maneuvered to the US Coast Guard station, and docked alongside a cutter.

The captain had the XO pick an armed team and go to the Coast Guard command center and see what they could find out. They returned an hour later with the commanding officer of the Coast Guard and his men. The XO had been able to use the telephone to call comsubpac for orders. They were to proceed to San Diageo where they would receive further orders, and equipment needed to repair the Coast Guards cutter. They also learned about what had happened and as how bad the communications were. That as far as anyone could tell that all satellites had either burnt up, flared off into space, or crashed to the earth. They were told that a few military vehicles were running and a few aircraft. That about all that was moving at sea was sail, and old analog ships. Those ships using fuel would only be able to get diesel, or coal it they were hauling food or other needed supplies.

...

Jack had just got home from visiting his son and grandkids when the power went out. He had an automatic generator, but that too was out. Jack looked up to his transformer, and saw that the fuse was not blown. He looked at his cell phone but it was dead. He then went inside the house and tried to call on his rotary dialed phone. He had always kept an old-style phone by his bed. If his power was out it would work so the power cooperative he worked for could get in touch with him and call him to work. Whatever was going on had to be really bad if it took out the land lines also. He and his wife Mary had food for several weeks. They had canned and put up plenty from his garden.

A couple days later, Buddy a kid he hardly recognized rode up on horseback. Buddy told him, Donnie wanted Jack to come back to work till this was over. They needed every lineman that could climb and knew the old switching methods to come in. Jack grabbed all his gear and loaded it onto his horse. A couple hours later he rode up to the main office of County Electric Cooperative.

A young lineman was sent out with each of the older retired linemen that had come in. As a team they went out on horseback and a foot to restore as much power as they could. They were to report in as they were able, to let dispatch know what they had been able to do. Totally against OSHSA and safety procedures, they would do switching without direct communication with dispatch. To maintain as safe a working environment as possible each team was sent to different substations. One team to each substation. This team and no one else were to be working on that section of line.

Each team had priority assignments to get on. Priority loads were medical centers, hospitals, fire stations, police stations, telephone, and communications. In reality, though the substation had to have power, then then main line out of the station. Then feeders off the main line before single phase and lateral lines could be gotten on. At each point would be a switch or fuse that had to be bypassed or perhaps refused. Then all newer transformers had aluminum winding which had melted. Many also had digital circuits that could have failed. In these situations, the transformer would have to be changed out before power to that consumer could be restored.

Jack and Jason started with the substation closest to both their homes. At the station, Jason confirmed that power was on to the station transformer. All of the three phase OCR's were open though. The control panels on each of these switches were digital. Jack smiled at Jason's despair, and told him it was simple enough. Jason was to manually open number one circuit, then with a long fiberglass pole open the bar switches to the OCR. Then with a very smooth and fast action close the bypass bar, on each phase. As each bar was closed they could hear the substation pick up the load. This procedure was followed with all four circuits coming off that substation.

Next Jason thought they would go south towards their homes checking the switches and getting what they could on, but Jack said, "no" they would go east back toward town. There was a medical clinic and a store, along with the telephones switch office on that line. As they went down the line they noticed some taps with open switches some going to oil fields or non-priority loads, which they took note of, but bypassed. A few they seen had fuses on small taps and they were on. Five miles down the line was an intersection and the line split three ways, each with an electronic switch. There was no power going through any of the switches. Going immediately to the switch feeding the town they manually opened and bypassed that switch.

From a quarter mile down the road they could hear people yelling excitedly with happiness. Smiling, they continued to the next switch. As they tried this switch they saw sparks and fire flying from atop a pole down that road. They opened it back up and rode down that way to see what was causing the problem. Nearly a mile down the line they spotted a pole with lightning arrestors which had blown up and the lead wires were tangled together. Jack pulled out his climbing gear and went up the pole to clear the wires. After they were able to get that section of line on to more cheers.

They worked like this for ten hours, and Jack said he had enough for one day. After a forty-minute ride he was home. He tried the rotary dial phone again and now it was working. Calling the office, he told them what they had got on and what he planned on doing the next day. He was told he needed to check the sub each morning and evening to make sure that they wouldn't overload it. There was only so much power available for the time and they may have to ration it to priority consumers.

By the time they had the main line of all four circuits on, dairies and nursing homes had been added to the priority list. Now they were getting power out on fairly long stretches of line. At a distance from the substations the voltage was dropping. Jack went to a regulator bank down line to check voltage. Here he found the voltage at 112 when it had been 125 at the substation. The regulator was on automatic and on down four. He moved it to manual and raised it to plus 2 at which point he had 124 volts.

That night when he called Donnie he informed him of the situation with the regulators. Donnie told him they had similar reports from every other crew. The biggest problem was that there were only two others that knew how to manually set and adjust regulators other than Jack. Donnie told Jack that the military had a couple of vehicles at their disposal to help and he would send one out for Jack tomorrow. Jack was to go around and manually monitor voltage, and make adjustments as needed. Jason would go with him, as it would be a good learning experience for him, and they would soon have another lineman that knew how to operate regulators.

The hydroelectric generators had not gone down. Some coal and gas fired were not to severally damaged. They were back on line in the first two weeks. The nuclear plants where another story. They had multiple digital controls which all had to be replaced. Wind farms needed mainly to have manual bypass switches closed in. Slowly power was being restored. As more power was added to the grid more load was being attached.

Jack and Jason now were starting each morning at dawn checking the substation. From there they would proceed down each circuit to regulator banks to check voltage, and make adjustments as needed. By dark they could go over three grids. The next day they would reverse their route. Thus, they would not be checking the same station or equipment at the same time each day. This helped to get a better idea of the total load management.

In the office other problems needed solved. With power being restored the need to meter usage and get readings. This had been done with smart meters, at every consumer. The smart meters no longer worked, nor did the repeaters which pushed their signal down the line. Either they would need to replace all meters with old style dial meters, and send someone out to read them, or repair all meters on site. What they did was something in between using old retired meters that were in storage they started changing out. The smart meters they brought in they worked around the clock to replace the circuit boards and test. All crews not still working on switching now changed meters.

Another problem was billing. All data on each consumer had been digitized on computer for years. Billing was calculated, and sent out by these computers, and the main frame at the office. Retired accountants and billing clerks where called in to manually on paper to handle billing. Old ledgers and documents had been stored in the basement these were used as a starting point for information. Needed parts, and electronics would have to be ordered and brought in from across the country. This was being repeated at every major utility.

Transporting was now a big concern. The US military was being used as much as possible to help with transportation, and the railways where starting to come back up. The diesel locomotives, for the most part needed but a few repairs to get running again.

CHAPTER 5

Bud Price was pampering his garden, to get as much out of it as possible. He had made arrangements, to sell all he and his neighbors could raise in Dallas. He would pull a trailer with his antique truck into town, loaded with vegetables. Unhappily his two granddaughters were weeding and helping each day. On Monday's his neighbors brought their produce to Buds house. There they all loaded the trailer and truck.

On their way into town a two police officers would met them and go with them to Dallas. As they entered Dallas other police officers on bicycles would join them. With their escorts they would proceed on the stores that were waiting on them. At the stores they traded for supplies they needed and cash. Then they would return home.

Bud did now have power and telephone service. He had tried to call Phoenix before, but hadn't any luck. This trip into Dallas he had spoken with one of the police officers which told him to try calling the police station in Phoenix at 6:00 pm. They were making provisions with them to get in touch with Bud's daughter, if possible. With great anticipation he and the entire family sat around the phone waiting for the correct time.

At six pm exactly Bud dialed the number that was given to him. Answering the phone on the other end was a police sergeant, who upon hearing who was calling said wait one minute. The next voice he heard was his granddaughters' mother, Debra. To say the least Debra was very joyful to hear from them. Debra told them that they were having to ration food in Phoenix. That her power was not on nor any phones other than the police and emergency services. She told her dad thanks for making sure she knew how to type and keep an old manual typewriter, due to this and that she could keep accounts on a ledger she was working several hours a day at different companies.

Knowing that the girls where ok she told them to do whatever their grandpa ask them, and that they might not be able to see each other for some time. Talking to her dad again she asked how he had made it possible for this call. It was totally unheard of. Bud told her about hauling food into Dallas and that the PD in Dallas had made the contact. She told him she wished he could haul food all the way out there but knew that wouldn't be possible for some time.

Bud told her to hang tough, that he was sure every farmer and small gardener was doing all they could to help out. Technology may be down for now but people in this country knew how to raise food and help each other in time of need. That they would take good care of the girls, and they would try to call again when they were able. He told her that the girls were helping with the garden and the fruit trees, and they had been helping grandma can food. What they really like best was the homemade jellies, and they were helping with canning the jelly.

Vegetables wasn't all they were able to sell in town. At times the farmers brought livestock into town to stores with butchers. They had an army escort for the days they brought in large loads and livestock. They now had two older tractors running which pulled trailers. They went into Dallas twice a week now once a week with a large convoy. Word had got out and many people lined the streets watching for them. When they pulled up to a store there would be a long line waiting for fresh food.

...

Colonel Colson was piloting a C130 to Kansas. He was to land at a small airport in Liberal. Once on the ground they would load him up with all sorts of food. Everything was going fine as there was very little flying these days. Which was good because communication was still very sporadic at best. With the best guess a southerly wind he approached the airfield from the south and buzzed the landing strip on the west side down the full length. Not seeing anything on the run way or that looked to be taxing he made a smooth turn around and prepared for a landing.

As he landed he saw an army Humvee with a private holding a follow me sign, so he followed them. They lead him to a warehouse. He pulled up near the open doors and spun the plane around to drop the back gate. Powering everything down he and his crew walked down the ramp to meet an army patrol and civilian authorities, along with some farmers.

Fuel was brought to the C130 as the cargo master supervised the loading of food and supplies from the warehouse. Colonel Colson went to the tower and visited with what officials were there. Loaded onto the aircraft was grain, corn, frozen beef, and pork, in cold containers.

Every inch of cargo space was packed tightly with much needed food.

There would be trains available soon which would be loaded and sent out, but right now there were a few cities in dire need of food. Using a map, a ruler and a compass Colonel Colson and his navigator would plot their course to Phoenix. Once the plane was fully loaded the captain returned to the tower where he was connected by phone to the tower in Phoenix. He informed them of his flight plan and eta. They said that the field would be clear at that time, and an army Humvee would direct him to his unloading point.

Telling everyone thank you, and goodbye he and his crew climbed back onboard. After firing up the engines, Colonel John Colson taxied to the far north end of the run way. He had a full load, although not as heavy as they could haul. He planned on using all the run way and take off as smooth as possible. Once airborne, and wheels up, he gently climbed to thirty thousand feet. Steering directly towards Phoenix, they would arrive in a couple hours. The flight was routine, and uneventful. As he approached Phoenix airport he again buzzed the field to see if the tarmac was clear. Seeing no obstruction, he slowly and smoothly landed. Finding the Humvee with a follow me sign again he followed to a group of army trucks.

Unloading was a breeze as the cargo master knew where everything was, and they had plenty of man power to unload. While this was going on, Colonel John went to the tower. There they told him that they had called Liberal to inform them, he had landed and was being unloaded. He asked to use the phone, and then John called his commanding officer for further orders. They would be flying to another Midwest town to load more food, for another hungry city.

That evening just before sun set, he landed in Amarillo, Texas. Here they spent the night and got a good sleep. Overnight the plane was loaded, fueled and ready at dawn. From here they went to Las Vegas. They unloaded in Las Vegas, and left for San Diageo empty.

In San Diageo they were refueled and loaded with engine parts for Navel and Coast Guard ships. They would have several stops to make, to deliver the equipment. First stop would be Las Angles, and then a layover in Hawaii.

...

Nathan rode his bicycle along with his partner. Today they would meet a convoy of food from the country and help guard if to the stores. Other officers would be at the stores and monitor the sales till the crowds dispersed. Riding down the street Nathan saw a mob of people with guns and clubs. Telling his partner to back him up from a distance he rode up to them. Calmly he tells them if they know of anyone that might want to take the food convoy they might let them know that the army was escorting the convoy now. Saying hope you can help me out he rode on to meet the convoy.

At the rendezvous point they meet the convoy right on time. Nathan went to the Army officer in charge. He informed him that there was a mob that looked like they might ambush the convoy. He also told him what he told them. The officer said that was very brave and resourceful. The officer had Nathan and his partner lead the convoy on to the first store. As they approached the place where he had seen the mob they saw only one guy watching them.

The rest of this patrol went very uneventful. After the last store, and drop off the army proceeded back to their base. The farmers started back toward their homes. Nathan rode in the direction of his home. On the street where he had seen the mob the same lone man was waving him down. The man told him thanks for the heads up.

"Ok what's up" asked Nathan.

I have a family and we are out of food. I'm a programing technician for a gaming corporation. The gaming business is a low priority so; I'm out of work for who knows how long. The stores are charging so much that we have run out of available cash.

"Where do you live", asked Nathan.

"I live a block south of here, on the left side of the road, forty three south Seventh Street," said the gentleman.

Nathan told him, he might have an idea for him. He would check it out and get back tomorrow. When Nathan got home he called the police department office. He gave them the report for the day's tour, and asked if they might have a position for a programmer. Since they had the digital replacements, they needed extra programmers for a few days. They told him to send his man in as soon as he could get there.

Oscar was surprised the next day, when Nathan came to his house. When, Nathan told him to go to the police office as soon, as he could for a possible short-term job, he left immediately. Walking the entire seven blocks, he hoped he would get the job and be able to buy food. Entering the station he asked for personnel. The office at the front desk wanted to know why he was there. He told them that officer Nathan had told him to come in about a possible job programming. Finding out that he was a programmer they sent him right back to the Captains desk. The Captain checked him out mostly to see if he would be trust worthy, with confidential information.

Oscar found himself in a cubical with a working desk top computer. The only connectivity was with other computers in the same building. They could stream high speed between each other with their hard connections. Connecting outside wasn't available, the only lines carrying a signal now was copper wires, which was to slow. With the operating systems they couldn't even load the opening page.

The best part of being back to work was they paid in cash at the end of each day. On his way home every afternoon he would stop by the market and purchase food to take home. They no longer had to worry about the next meal. They still had no idea about their family in Oklahoma, whether they were even ok. No one

they knew had been able to find out anything
from outside the neighborhood.

...

Richard Prater and Robert Scott had a
complete crop growing in the hot house. They
had assembled the hot house soon after arriving
on Mars. They used their own waste for fertilizer,
and soil from the Martian surface. Seeds
unloaded off the supply ship, and planted
carefully. In a few months these would not only
provide their food, but also help with oxygen
supply.

Mark and Janice White prepared the living
habitat, while the hot house was being arranged.
Emily Prater, Jacob Wells, Lea Marten, and Dan
Freeman worked in the Laboratory habitat. Here
they not only had a full laboratory, but a clinic,
and communications facility. In the center of the
facility was a multiport computer station. Five
seats in front of five computers, each with
screens, arranged around a large three-
dimensional screen in a way that any information
could be placed for all to see.

Practically all the data from NASA was in their
main frame. They now probably had more saved
data than what was available on Earth. Before
the solar flare data could have been streamed
with a high-speed data burst, though they could
send no one on Earth could receive.

Together they had assembled the habitats, and
started mining for ice. They had set up solar
panels for power, with inverters to keep their

batteries charged. They had seven year batteries in all their gear, with backup replacements. They had wind generators which had been set up. In the first few weeks through hard work they now had a regular colony underway.

Twice a day Jacob would check the recorder for incoming messages from Earth. The second message from Earth he received had a report on how the Earth was doing. They also heard from some of their families. His wife Amy and kids lived in Houston, and had been easy to get hold of. They were doing ok, and NASA was seeing to their needs. Lea Martin's, father was in South Carolina, and was doing fine.

They had not been able to get any word from Richard, and Emily Prater's families, which lived in the state of Washington. Mark White had no immediate family other than Janice. Janice's mother and father in Alabama were ok. Robert Scott's mother lived in Hawaii, and there had been no communication to or from Hawaii. Dan Freeman was divorced and had no one else.

Lea had collected several mineral samples, and was analyzing them in the lab. Right off she had found that the surface dust was heavy laden with iron ore. Another abundant element discovered so far was silicon. She was very excited about the future possibilities of research.

The colony had the 3D printer set up and operating. An Ultimaker 7 maximum, with it they could use most any raw material to produce many of the material they needed. First the colony fashioned 3D frustums, with which they could build permanent habitats. These habitats were built like igloos with interconnecting tunnels. Each tunnel with air tight accesses at either end. The base of each building was dug out eight feet below the surface and the tunnels too were below ground. The matter that was dug out of the trenches between the habitats, was used to feed the 3D printer.

Eight people working together with an impulsive fervor, were able to accomplice much in a short time. Though their situation wasn't desperate yet, they each knew that survival depended on every one's cooperation, and dedicated hard work. Each morning over breakfast Mark conducted a meeting planning out the day's tasks, and by what method they needed to be completed safely. Each night they crawled into their sleeping racks exhausted from the day's work.

The daily temperature could range from 75 degrees down to minus 100 degrees. The gravity on Mars is approximately thirty eight percent of Earth thereby everything weighed just over one third of what it would on earth. Pressure was also a main concern. Only about a 1 percent pressure of Earth, pressure suits must be worn at all times except inside pressurized habitats.

As the work progressed, breaks were scheduled for the colonist. In teams of two or three they would explore the area. On such expeditions they would collect soil samples, along with mapping the expanse. They would also use a hand boring tool to take samples from a few feet below the surface. Rock and mineral samples were collected from the mountains. All samples were taken back to the lab for analysis.

Over a period of time a comprehensive map was made of the entire region. At more than one location diamonds had been discovered. At different locations gold, and other precious minerals were found.

After one such excursion Lea came down with a server rash. Quickly the rash turned to sores, and spread. Lea was isolated immediately and Dr. Elizabeth Prater began treating her. Richard Prater, and Robert Scott was called to the lab to analyze samples from Lea's skin to determine the cause. After many hours of work, they decided it was an allergy to the very fine dust that covers Mars. So fine is the dust that it managed to get into everywhere, including their pressure suits. A treatment was produced, and soon Lea was back to her happy self. Before Lea was healthy again, Jason came down with the same rash. He too was healed. If was quickly ascertained that once a person had the rash and was healed, they were immune from getting it again. Over the next few weeks each person on the colony had experienced the rash to one degree or another.

Discussion often included Earth, and the time they would need to decide whether or not to return. The more the colony advanced the less any talked of returning to Earth. Every week that passed the more certain that the colony was self-sufficient. After several months Earth regular broadcast informed them that electronics were being replaced with new post flare parts. They were also informed that at optimal launch date that the colony should consider returning to Earth.

The colony decided that the return trip would have to be made, but not necessarily by the whole team. Each person would need to make their own decision as to whether or not they wished to return. If a colony was to stay on Mars certain personnel would have to stay. Mark held a list as to the needed requirements of skills for the colony to continue. Without the personnel possessing these skills then all should return. Mark did not disclose this to any other, not even his wife Janice. Mark intended for everyone to decide truly on their own. It was determined that they had until two months before optimal launch time before a decision was necessary. Earth was informed that at least some if not all would return, but they would continue on with permanent colony construction till that time.

At the next scheduled communication with Earth, they were informed that among items to bring back would be all data within their computers. So much had been lost that the information they had was of vital importance. They were also told that many of the technological components were being rebuilt and communication had pretty much been restored across the world. With the information in their computers in two of three years another trip to Mars might be possible.

Although it was considered not worth the effort to send gold to Earth, perhaps jewelry fashioned on Mars would be of great value. Lea, and Robert set about designing and making a few pieces to send back to Earth. What and who ever did return the combined weight had to be pains takingly calculated, and observed.

During the night Janice told her husband Mark that if he wished to stay on Mars she too would stay. When Mark confirmed what she was already sure of Janice then told him that at tomorrows meeting both Richard and Emily Prater intended to announce their intentions to remain on Mars.

Laying in each other's arms, Lea and Robert also discussed remaining on Mars. Lea said that Emily had told her she wished to stay, as had Janice. Robert then asked Lea if she would marry him. Lea smiled and said she would if he could find a preacher or even a justice of the peace. Robert told her he had already thought of that, and as captain and colony leader Mark would be qualified to perform a marriage. "At breakfast tomorrow let's tell everyone," said Lea.

At the table the next morning Robert proclaimed I have an announcement. As it became quiet, he announced that he and Lea were to be married as soon as possible. After all the congratulations were given, Mark told the team that he and Janice planned to remain on Mars. The Praters also exclaimed their intentions to stay. Robert and Lea too gave their intentions to stay. Jacob said that he would return to Earth only if the colony could manage without him. That left it up to Dan who said that it made since for the married couples to stay on Mars and the two bachelors to return to Earth.

Jason and Dan both expressed desires to return to Mars if able someday. As a message was being prepared to send to Earth, this desire to return was articulated adamantly. That priority consideration should be given to Jacob and Dan, if they so desired. Thus, plans were put into motion for Alpha to return to Earth. Skills of the two men returning to Earth that the colony needed were taught to one or another of the ones staying.

CHAPTER 6

On their way up the mountain Craig showed Melinda where to find wild onions, and edible berries. At night he taught her how to find dry wood and start a fire. Later they snuggled together around the fire and wondered at, how great life was. Though their days were filled with hard work preparing for winter, their life was filled with love and joy.

Game was killed, their fur made into coats and blankets. Meat was smoked and froze in the ice. Firewood was gathered and stacked near the cave entrance. All to soon winter came on as it normally does at this high an altitude, in the Rockies. Their main task during the long months of winter was to keep the fire going, collect water, and eat. For the water sometimes, they would have to melt ice over the fire for drinking water.

They grew to love each other more each passing day. By midwinter it was obvious to both of them that Melinda was pregnant. They would lay around the fire while Craig would read to her. Melinda loved to hear Craig read as he would articulate each sentence. Melinda being young, healthy, and very happy was blessed with a gentle pregnancy. Their best guess at the arrival time was around the middle of May. The passes wouldn't be clear of snow till late April or early May so they planned on going down the mountain as soon as the passes were open enough to allow them easy access. They figured on staying in town till Melinda, and the baby were strong enough to come back up the mountain.

Craig intended to take all the extra smoked meat and furs down to Dubois to trade. Anything edible was worth much in trade now. He had managed to pan a little gold, this too he would take down to trade. Once he got Melinda down and safe, he might have to make another trip to get everything down.

As the days became longer and warmer, they started finding more game. The lower valley had edible mushrooms growing. In the spring fresh water cress grew. Craig would go out to hunt and Melinda would go pick water cress, or mushrooms. Craig would argue with Melinda about her going out, but she told him the walk would do her and the baby good.

One day they were together above the tree line when they saw an airplane going overhead. It was the first plane they had seen since the flare. They had noticed that the air was much cleaner than it had been in their lifetime. At night the stars were brilliant. The moon was so visible that they could almost make out the mountains with bare eyesight. They had noticed that at night more and more towns had lights on.

By the end of April, the passes were clear enough for them to start down the mountain. Craig wouldn't let Melinda carry anything even with her protest. Craig carried all they needed for the journey, and what trade items he could on his back. Craig watched Melinda closely, and with any sign of fatigue, he would claim to be tired and need a break. On the second afternoon Melinda told Craig she was doing fine and if he didn't stop taking so many breaks, she would carry the backpack. Not long after near Elk Lake they saw a truck on one of the few trails that came half way up the mountain. Walking across a small clearing they saw Brian, one of the towns folk Craig had met in Dubois.

Brain had been fishing, and was tearing down his camp to go home. Brian was happy to give them a ride into Dubois. A couple hours later they were in town and in Gary's home resting. A doctor had been called and was on the way to check out Melinda. Gary offered to drive Craig up as far as possible to carry down the other furs and meat. Though some food stuff was getting through and some locals had been hunting and fishing, food was greatly appreciated. They waited till the doctor had examined Melinda and assured them it would be at least two to three weeks before the baby would come, before Craig decided to go back up the mountain. The doctor had also told them that Melinda and the baby were both doing great.

Craig and Gary left early in the morning two days later. Driving a truck as far as they could they then drove farther with a gator ATV. By dark they were at the cave and had the ATV loaded ready to go back down. They talked of the flare and how the town was doing, and about how Melinda and Craig had been doing up on the mountain. They went back to Dubois the next day arriving before dark.

...

Colonel John Colson was flying nearly ever day. Often as not hauling food, if not then badly needed supplies. Today he was carrying digital components to NASA in Florida. There he would load produce to haul to New York City. He now was flying more hours and back to back trips than was allowed on commercial air.

John had learned that his ex-wife and children were ok in Boston. Since he was going to the north east for the first time since the flare, John asked for a couple days leave to see his kids. He was given four days while his c130 had its regular overhaul.

A few electric trains and subways were running again so John was easily able to catch a ride to Boston, especially since he was wearing his Air Force uniform. In Boston transportation wasn't as easy, but since it was only nine blocks, he walked to Jenifer's house. John had called from New York and told them he was coming and about what time he should arrive. John wasn't surprised that the door was opened when he knocked, but he was shocked at the reception he received. Jenifer rushed to him and hugged him tightly.

"What brought that on, though I'm not complaining," said John.

"Just we all missed you so much and have been worried sick about you. We have heard a little about what has happened and we heard about your crash," said Jenifer. "I read in the paper that you are a hero, landing that plane with so many lives saved. How long can you stay, and will you stay with us?"

John was still amazed at how warm she felt in his arms. Jenifer's long shiny red hair reminded him of the sunset. Again, as when they had first made love her kisses were hot and passionate. The fire that was there years ago had returned with intensity.

Over the next three days Jenifer told him she was wrong to leave him and she missed him. John explained that since he was flying wherever the Air Force sent him, he had no schedule, nor any idea when he might be able to return to Boston. He would probably be around much less, till the emergency was over.

When Colonel John returned to his aircraft his crew noticed a change in John's expression. They kept at him wanting to know how his leave was until he finally acknowledged that he and his wife had got back together. With a good number of trains now in operation, the priority shipments for them was tech. The overall expectation for a return to normalcy was a year and a half to two years. Solid state circuits were being built around the clock. These circuits then needed to be transported to the needed locations as soon as possible.

NASA in Florida, and SCAMI both needed replacement circuit boards, and digital components. They had plans to replace needed satellites as fast as they could. Launch's would begin within a month and continue as fast, and as long as necessary. The first would be communications and GPS. SCAMI was also working around the clock on a ship to make a round trip to Mars. That would take many months to complete.

After a few more trips back, and forth across the nation hauling needed freight, they were order to a meeting in Dayton Ohio. Arriving at Patterson Air Force Base Colonel John Colson whistled at the number of cargo planes on the tarmac. Once they had shut everything down, they were escorted to a briefing room full of other crews.

The word was that regular Air Force would continue for a while hauling freight while Guard and Reserve units would be rotated out. They were informed that some commercial airlines would be back in service before long, and would be needing their pilots back. They were also offered a ride as available to the locations of their choice.

John made a phone call to Jenifer as soon as the meeting was dismissed telling her he would be catching a ride to Boston as soon as he was able. Then he called his airline to see if and or when they might need him. John was informed that he could report in within the week at their New York office.

...

Jack was fatigued, working ten-hour days, six days a week was a young man's task. He had retired for just that reason. Donnie could tell that the older lineman they had brought in were wearing down. Donnie called them all in for a meeting. He told them that they really appreciated their hard work, and they could start winding down the number of work hours. He also told them that as the younger lineman learned the manual techniques, and as the digital devices came back online, the retired lineman would be payed a large bonus and they could all return to their homes.

Once the entire system was back online the main concern was metering and load control. As replacement components arrived for the regulators, the control panels had to be changed out. Jack had started letting Jason bypass the regulators under his supervision. The most important thing to know in bypassing a voltage regulator Jack told Jason was to always be sure it was in the neutral position before closing the bypass switch.

If the bypass switch was closed with the line and source switch closed, and the regulator was in any position other than neutral it would explode violently. Several gallons of boiling oil, and several pounds of molten copper would fall of you in microseconds. There was three ways to be certain that the regulator was in neutral position. One was a neutral light on the control board. Second was a position indicator on the side of the regulator. The third was to manually step the regulator up or down and count the steps from one end to the other and center on sixteen steps. Jack informed Jason that he needed to always be sure of at least two method's before closing the third switch.

Jack knew that Jason was well trained as a lineman, and Jason knew the new technological systems. Now Jason was becoming capable in the old techniques of a lineman. These ways hadn't been used in years, but now they had saved the cooperative.

New circuit boards for the smart meters were starting to arrive and again the meter personnel were changing out the meters. They would start on one circuit out of a substation and the lineman would restore the repeaters, then the meter personnel would change all the meters, on that circuit. Before this was even started the computers had to be repaired, or replaced, and tested. As each system was put online it would be tested and checked before proceeding to the next section.

Circuit boards for their vehicles were replaced after police and emergency service's. Auto service centers started receiving the parts to repair cars and trucks if they had the ability to go out in the field to do so. The auto repair crews were monitored to make certain they worked on priority vehicles first.

Jack was getting ready to leave his house to go to the office, when he heard a truck pull into the drive. Looking out Jack smiled as he saw Jason driving the basket truck. No more climbing poles for them he thought. After a few more days working with Jason, Jack informed Donnie that Jack was capable to work alone and could handle any switching situation. Donnie and the cooperative thanked Jack for helping out in the time of need and let Jason drive him home.

...

Bud and the family had continued to work the gardens and put away preserves. Bud had started cutting firewood and getting ready for winter. They now had electricity and telephone service on the land line. Today he saw workers at cell phone tower on the hill near the main highway. On his next trip into town he stopped by the telephone company's office with all their cell phones in pocket. After giving his name and account of his and the granddaughters, he was told that he was authorized for two cell phones only, at this time. Since he was bringing food to town one had to be his. Bud had to pay to replace his cell and he paid to replace one of the girl's cell phones.

When Bud got back home, he presented the working cell phone to his granddaughters. They would have to share it and together they had very limited calls and no data for the time. The girls were extremely happy just to have a working device.

As service's started returning the demand for working devices became a top problem. Out of work techie's opened shops to repair burnt out cells, computers, and televisions. Components were hard to come by at first, but as priority needs were met, more units were made available.

After much begging and bribery Penny, and Peggy talked their grandfather into taking a television in to see if it could be fixed. Bud found Oscar who had finished with the police department and now had a shop set up in his garage. Oscar checked the set over and told Bud he would try to get the parts needed for it, but it might take a few weeks. He also told him that the only broadcasts as of yet was local over the air. A price was agreed upon, and Bud promised to return in a couple weeks to check on progress.

The use of money had again resumed. The banks were open and accounting by ledger had been in use for months. Computers were being replaced or repaired, and the institutions slowly were returning to normal. Bud went to the bank and deposited the funds from his sale of produce. He kept enough to purchase the things his family needed. Check writing had again become a way of life. As in years past, excepting checks was a sign of trust. Someone unknown was hard pressed to have a check accepted.

In the few months Penny, and Peggy had grown strong not only in body but in mind too. They now showed initiative. They would arise early in the mornings, and do the chores assigned to them without being told. If they saw a task needing done, they would tackle it if able. The day came their mother called, and had made arrangements for them to come home to Arizona. Tickets had been bought for them on a train going from Ft Worth to Phoenix. Only a few passenger cars were available on the rails yet, but to return minor children to their parents' exceptions were made.

When they arrived home their mother and father hardly recognized them. Their father called them his little ladies. Their parents were astonished at the abilities the girls now possessed. They would jump up from dinner to wash dishes. When Debra was cooking, they would be there to help. One day Penny saw a rabbit in the yard and threw a rock hitting it in the head. She then cleaned the rabbit and had it ready for dinner that night.

...

Bethany watched Nathan sleeping. He had worked a double shift, and been sleeping for nearly ten hours. Reed kept asking for his daddy to get up and play with him. Looking back at Nathan from a book she was reading Bethany's eye meet her loving husbands' eyes. They smiled at each other and reached out to touch hands. Nathan gently pulled her to him as she removed her robe. The hot sweaty passion of their love making reinvigorated their devotion to each other. Afterwards they showered together and while doing so made love again.

When Nathan returned to duty, he was driving his squad car. Though he did have radio he did not have a working on board computer. He could call dispatch and they did have computers again and some data restored. Most records of criminal past were available. The roads for the most part was open now though many abandon cars still cluttered the right of way. Traffic was very light so travel was easy. Many on Nathan's beat knew him now and respected his way. Nathan had treated everyone with respect, and compassion, and the word had spread. This is the kind of law enforcement that Nathan had read about and desired to be a part of.

On any given day people would talk to Nathan, tell him what was going on. In other places a police officer had little respect or help, but Nathan could count on his neighbors, as they could count on him. Report of Nathan's account had reached the Dallas Police Departments headquarters. Many had herald Nathan as a hero of justice. Today while on patrol Nathan was called on the radio to go to city hall, immediately.

Reaching the building Nathan was handed his own dress uniform and informed he needed to get into it now. Not asking questions he went in a restroom and changed. In his best dress uniform Nathan was led to the council chambers. Upon entering the chambers, he notices the newspaper and television news there. As he approached the front, he could see the mayor, and his chief, he also saw Bethany holding Reed. Nathan was awarded the departments highest award, and given a promotion to Lieutenant.

The Chief reassigned him to training and sent him to each precinct to train all officers his technique. The Mayor not only told them that he was proud of Nathan, but he was the type of police officer that he wished all officers were like. After the ceremony the press was eager to talk to Nathan. When asked what it was that he did differently, he told them that he just treated everyone as he would like to be treated himself. Even those he arrested he treated with dignity, and compassion.

In a private meeting later with the chief of police Nathan said he wasn't sure he wanted to leave a street beat. The Chief told him that was the reason they really needed him to train others to be as effective as he had been. They also wanted him to oversee police one. Their version of oversight and enforcement. It was high time that law enforcement was for the people and all the people. He wanted a police force that was the envy of every city across the nation.

That evening Nathan went home to his family with doubt of his ability to preform all that was expected of him. Bethany expressed her confidence that he was very able to handle the appointment.

Nathan started off with the largest precinct first thing the next morning. At their morning assembly, he showed up unannounced. As he walked to the front, he received a standing ovation. Motioning everyone to sit he proclaimed he was undeserving their adoration. Then he told them from today on they were to look for ways they could serve the community. Their job wasn't to police the public, but to serve the public. Treating everyone with respect and compassion lead to a more informative public, and better public relations.

Within a week the image of the Dallas Police Department had improved significantly. In some ways a return to the past's ways, had proven beneficial to all. Technology can be a great advantage, but total dependence upon anything can be very detrimental. This too had been a terrible lesson in the last few months. The world would return to its high-tech ways in time, but the cost came dearly. Many lives had been lost; and those that lived had their lives disrupted in ways never imagined.

CHAPTER 7

Dr. Talbert was busy planning for the return of Alpha and her two-man crew to Earth. He was also involved with the placement of the communications satellites, being launched as rapidly as possible. New multi tasked satellites were being developed for deployment. Satellites that not only could be used for cell phones, but also television, and GPS. The military had their own requirements, but fortunately the Air Force had its own capabilities to launch, and they only knew what was launched.

Beta the name of the ship to go back to Mars was on schedule. It would be larger, designed and built by SCAMI, but overseen by NASA, on request. Dr Talbert had the opportunity to go to Florida to inspect it once, and would again before it's launch. SCAMI was insistent on sending another group of colonists to Mars on the return trip. The official response was to wait and see how the crew on Mars was doing before sending more.

SCAMI had started looking for those with the right skills and a desire to migrate. Those willing would be trained, and held in a standby post tell further notice. Training included all knowledge of the current situation on Mars, and expected changes. How to repair any and all equipment that was essential to the needs of the Colony. Each prospective colonist was enlightened to the fact that they would be the second crew to Mars. The first colonist had been there for nearly three years by the time they would get there. The original colonist would by the governing body for Mars.

The number of colonists to make the trip was determined to be twenty. The first two confirmed was, Jacob Wells, and Dan Freeman. It was also expected that they might wish to take someone with them, so a place was reserved for possible spouses. For all other than the two from the original team the trip would cost, and the price would be great. SCAMI was a corporation after all, and its future depended on profits. So far, this adventure had been very costly, but the opportunity for great profit often required great expenses.

Dr Talbert and Carl had worked with SCAMI executives to reestablish communications directly to SCAMI office with the Mars Colony. Regular communication was needed to prepare for the resupply and reinforcement of the colony. Those on Mars would have to continue at a stringent pace to prepare for the others coming. More habitats would have to be built and made ready. More green houses started for food and oxygen. Much more ice for water.

Once SCAMI had a private connection with Mars, Chris the executive vise president in charge of the Martian colony, sent a secure message. The original colonist was each given stock in the colony, but not enough that they could override SCAMI. By giving them stock SCAMI hoped to control the colony. The uppermost priority for the corporation was to make a profit.

On Mars they had found a large vein of a unique gold, that was bright red. Although of great value on Earth the cost of transportation was prohibitive of a profit. Ideas had formed with the colonist as to possible use of the gold. One was jewelry made on Mars. The other was for them to make digital circuits using the gold. There was silicon aplenty, but schematics for the equipment was needed. This they proposed to the SCAMI executive Chris.

Chris took the idea to the research and development department, and everything the colony would need was added to the load out plan for Beta. Chris informed the colony that they were sending the needed elements for them to make solid state electronics. He also told them that SCAMI had set up an account for each of them at the bank. They would each have a large sum of money in their accounts. SCAMI would pay them a bonus for the items shipped back to Earth.

All this was a way to maintain tight control of Mars, or so the executives of SCAMI thought at the time. Much later on this was to come back on them, but that is another story for another time.

...

At the morning breakfast meeting, Janice asked Emily if she had time to do a physical. Emily smiled and said sure thing right after the meeting. During the meeting discussion of their pending wealth back on Earth. Robert pointed out the fact that money on Earth would probably be of little value to their needs on Mars.

Leah also opened the dialogue that SCAMI expected them to form a governing body, before the arrival of more colonist. It was proposed by Emily and confirmed by all that as he had been their leader from the first day of training that Mark should be named Governor of Mars. Part of his immediate duties was to include writing out laws for the colony. That everything propositioned would be brought before this group for ratification. Since everyone agreed and Emily had brought the idea forward, she was to be the chairperson for the committee.

Later this committee would become the Mars Congress. A constitution would be written and provisions for electing of representatives. This would take ten years to come to completion.

In the clinic Emily confirmed what Janice was already certain of, that she was pregnant. The colony would have their first native born citizen. Emily then told Janice that she too was expecting, but not as far along as Janice. Together they made plans for the births of their children. Emily would of course deliver Janice's baby, and would learn to help Emily with her delivery.

Together they sat at the next mornings meal, and meeting. Janice usually had little to say at these meetings, but today she spoke out with the news of her pregnancy. As everyone cheered and applauded, she waved to hush them. Pointing to Emily, all became silent. Then Emily announced that she too was pregnant. After many cheers Mark announced a day of rest, a one-time holiday in recognition of the wonderful announcement.

After their first holiday the team went back to work with vigor. Digging foundations for the new habitats, and tunnels. Building more greenhouses for food. Securing more ice for water, and solar collectors. In the process of searching for more ice sources Leah discovered a cave not to far from the base.

Exploring the cavern, they found pure fresh water deep down inside one of the tunnels. There were only two openings to the cave, one was large and just behind a rock outcrop. The other was higher up the mountain, and fairly small. A plastic tarp which had been used for part of the temporary habitat was used to close off the openings. Then an atmospheric pump was brought to the cave to attempt to pressurize the cavern. At first it didn't seem to be working, but after a few days the cavern was pressurized. The cave was left for two weeks and then tested to see if it had held the same pressure or if there were a leak.

Janice White went with Robert Scott to more closely explore the cave. She was hoping to find some indication that intelligent life had been there before. Looking for writing or drawings on the walls of the cave. Robert was taking samples from the water and soil, and well as scrapings from the cavern walls hoping to find any sign of life, present or past. What they found, was nothing, no indication of any sort of life.

The decision was made by the committee to maintain the cave as a community area for the colony. Part of the research was intensive study of seismic activities. Until a full understanding of the likelihood of a possible quake moving into a cave was to be considered risky at best. Still if the use of the cave became reasonable then it would be a valuable resource for the colony.

The entrance to the cave was inside a nearly round crater. By using prism shaped building blocks, they could seal the entire crater. They would build a top over the crater much like an igloo. These blocks they could manufacture with the 3D printer. The blocks would be so smooth that when placed together they would seal air tight with the pressure holding them in place. In time they could totally enclose the crater, and pressurize it along with the cave.

The discoveries they had made and the resources found had all been within fifteen miles of the base camp and landing site. As they were getting settled in and caught up on survival needs, they began relaxing into a routine. All work and no play would become taxing way to soon, so they had relief in the evenings. Card games, and or chess, as well as other activities. Reading was a favorite pass time, which they had a complete library reduced to a flash drive.

Venturing further from base camp was a difficult task as provision had to be made for a long term stay away from the colony. Enough air and battery reserve were just a couple of the concerns for such a trip. To accurately map the area expanded expeditions were required. On one such excursion to a known crater Leah and Robert Scott were checking it for a possible location to one day build a spaceship launch facility.

Richard Prater's sister Rebecca, was a financial planner with an accounting degree. He and Emily had arranged for her to take care of their assets on Earth. The rest of the colony decided to have Rebecca manage all their funds too. Rebecca reinvested in SCAMI and other tech funds. The holdings for the Mars Colony grew rapidly.

...

Back on Earth, in New York City, Tom Backster was again working. When trading had first resumed, he needed five accountants and assistants to keep track of trades. Later as computers were repaired or replaced these assistants were required to program the software he needed. The early trades Tom made were on the floor. He was accustomed to trading online, but enjoyed the vitality of live trades.

The economy and all life were slowly returning to some resemblance of normalcy. It would take several years to totally recover but the world was recovering. The loss of life had been substantial yet the reduced food supplies had correlated with that loss. In locations with lighter loss of life, hunger was worse. Although difficult the people of Earth overcame the disaster. Hurricanes, tsunamis, and earthquakes had conditioned the populace for this the worst event in modern history.

The restoration of technology did not concern all on the planet though. In Dubois Wyoming Craig and Melinda was only concerned with the birth of their son, Jim. Named Jim after the most famous mountain man Jim Bridger. The birth went smoothly and both mother and son were in great shape. Their plan was to remain in the town for a few weeks before going back up the mountain.

Gary talked daily with Craig trying to convince him to stay in Dubois as his deputy. Craig spoke to Melinda about the offer but neither wished to remain in civilization. Melinda told Craig she was happier than she had ever been with him on the mountain. All they needed was each other and what the mountain could provide for them.

While in town they had heard the stories of how difficult it was and had been for everyone. With no digital devices they had not missed a thing. Even the lowest tech elder had missed their cell phone service. Most people had totally been at a loss for weeks without being connected to the world wide web. Some where not able to find their way around town without GPS tracking. They were at an awe of how devastated some people were of the loss of simple devises. For them only the loss of someone dear to them would cause such anguish.

With no regret the three of them soon started their long hike back up their mountain. Craig carrying his heavily laden back pack and his son in a forward-facing infant carrier. Though it had been three weeks since giving birth, Craig wouldn't let Melinda carry anything. Though Melinda complained about Craig carrying everything, she loved him all the more for his chivalry.

Just over two days later they arrived at their cave. It took another two days for them to get completely set back up into their normal routine. Again, hunting and fishing became the labor of life for them. Stitching clothing from cured hides in preparation for winter, was main concern. In the cities people made their selves sick over stressful multi million, dollar decisions, but here they had no such stress. Even on occasion they saw a mountain lion or bear, this was of little stress as they knew how to get along with them. They were not an easy prey for either. They both always carried a gun and both could use it, though they seldom needed to.

Winter came and they were happy and warm in their cave. The fire was kept blazing day and night. They ate and cuddled together. Daily they would take turns reading out loud so that Jim could hear and learn. They also sang together, because Melinda told Craig that singing to a child enhanced intelligence. As spring came, they discussed whether or not they really needed to go down the mountain. Their lives were becoming less tied to the outside world.

...

John Colson was in a captain uniform with the airline company he had worked with before the flare. Now he had an international route to London spend the night and return to New York the next day. He would then have two days off then repeat the same trip. Though he wasn't flying a new 787 yet he was piloting a very familiar 737. He and Jenifer were both extremely pleased with his new work schedule. As soon as he arrived back in New York he would be able to catch a train to Boston and be with his family.

A little over a week after resuming his job with the airline John and Jenifer were married, again. This time it would be for good, as they were both fully committed to a lasting relationship. Whatever faced them they could endure it together.

The week after their wedding John was called in for a meeting. He was given a special assignment. This trip would go to Chicago, then to Denver, then on the LA. From LA they would go to DFW, and then to Miami. All told they would only have twenty passengers. These were the twenty colonist which were going to Miami to prepare to go to Mars. John had been selected to pilot the aircraft transporting them because he was considered a hero, and because of his rank and security clearance with the Air Force.

For this trip and thereafter he would be piloting a brand new 787. One of the holdups getting them into service had been the deployment of necessary GPS satellites. The 787 used state of the art tracking systems to monitor its location for navigation. This particular unit had over twenty first class seats and their special passengers would be flying first class.

After an uneventful trip Captain Colson landed in Miami. There he was allowed to meet the entire crew of colonist. Jacob Wells was returning to Mars with wife Julia whom he had known since grade school. Julia was a computer programmer, and hardware technician. Dan Freeman was also returning with a wife Amy. She was a renowned chef and exceptional organizer.

Benjamin and Connie Baker, he is a top construction specialist and she is a jewel smith. The rest of the team was not married though there was an equal number of females to male, members. Tyler Lee, though not an expert at any one thing was very capable in task put in front of him. Tyler was also an ordained minister, and councilor with a phycology degree. Tyler also had worked nights as a bar tender, saying he enjoyed listening to people's problems. William Taft not only had a military back ground making him capable with any weapon, he also had a law degree.

Lisa Thurman had intensive expertise in micro design engineering. Her passion was micro robotics. Sheila Anderson is the best Mycologist in the field. Sheila was tasked with starting a growth of environmentally controlled edible mushrooms. Carlita Santos trained as a chemical engineer.

Brea Johnson was a mathematical genius with degrees from MIT and Princeton. She was expert in everything from nuclear physics to astronomy.

Brea would lead the effort to build and operate a space port. Unknown to any even at SCAMI Brea had years earlier purchased stock in the SCAMI corporation.

David Goldberg was with research and development. Seth Lane was a muscle-bound laborer that never seemed to tire. Kevin Peters was highly trained in climate control. Randy Mason was very good at masonry, or any other form of putting things together. Derrick Jackson had degrees in geology and electrical engineering. Derrick had been working in the energy field for the last five years. Charles Thomas was a farmer or so he called himself. He had a degree in agronomy and could grow anything anyplace.

Debbie Hart wasn't sure how she had been selected, though she had volunteered early she didn't have a degree or any specialty. Debbie did have a very useful talent for the colony though, she could knit, weave, and sew just about anything. Thereby she would be able to keep clothing for the colony. She was also very good with children, which would prove handy soon after their arrival.

Salina Gonzales studied at Cal Tec and graduated with honors in digital electronics design engineering. A large title to say she could design and build a circuit for any task. Amanda Brown had a degree in drafting and architecture.

Their training would include the use, and maintenance of their pressure suits. The current design of the Mars Colony, and the necessity to maintain a sealed atmosphere. They were advised about the rash the first colonist each experienced, and that they might as well except the fact they too would suffer from it. One of the most important lessons was to expected the totally unexpected. The unknown was very likely to happen in a completely alien location. The most important trait in each candidate had been an ability to work with others, and a willingness to do so under the most stressful environment imaginable.

By the time this team was at NASA training for Mars, word had come of the first birth on Mars. Mother and daughter were fine. During joyous celebrations at SCAMI office the FEO joking stated they should figure a way to tax the colonist for births. Though joking that seemed to be the mentality of the corporate office, controlling the Colony. Expectations were high for a successful birth of a second child in a month and a half.

SCAMI had collected from each colonist going to Mars. A Deal to deduct their earnings had been made with Dan and Jacob. For a long time to come making a return trip to Earth would be a very costly ticket. For the trip to and back from Mars on Beta there would be a pilot and engineer which would go and return. On the return trip hopes were high that again they would be loaded with valuable articles which would provide a profit for the corporation.

The pilot Terry Palmer and engineer Betty Woods would also make the next trip in an even larger ship. Hopefully caring up to fifty paying colonists. Very little space or weight allowance would be made for freight from Earth to Mars, but the return trip had room for items which would provide a profit.

One of the biggest issues needed for discovery and development was rocket fuel. If a source could be found on Mars this would lower the expense and thereby raise the profit margin for the corporation. It would also be another source of trade for the colony.

CHAPTER 8

At Houston's NASA's space control Dr Talbert had just overseen the launch of a rocket from Florida which would place three satellites in orbit. Minutes before a launch from a secrete Air Force base in Nevada had also placed unknown satellites in orbit. Though he and his team could see their launch they had no control or further information on it. All they knew for sure was that it would not be close enough to their craft to pose a problem.

Dr. Raymond Talbert had also been involved in the preparations for the upcoming launch of the Beta craft to Mars. Raymond truly wished he could be one of the colonists going. He had spoke many times with his wife Jessica about the prospect, and she too was interested in going. Hanna their daughter was very doubtful though. She was very upset at the prospect of losing all her friends, and about never getting to play softball again. Hanna did like the idea of adventure and a totally new way of life.

In a week Dr Talbert had to fly to Florida for a meeting with the launch personnel and with the team of Beta. While in Florida Raymond asked to have his family put on the candidate list for the next colonization voyage. With little surprise Raymond's superiors explained that if he was selected and could afford the ticket, he would be greatly missed. Then it was concurred that his talent would be of equally great value on Mars. The leadership at NASA concluded that his research capabilities would be enhanced on Mars, and he would be able to communicate his discoveries back to them.

When Dr Raymond Talbert and family came across the candidate list at SCAMI, they were delighted to add his name at the top of the list. This list was stamped unpaid. As the candidates paid for their ticket their names were placed on the final list of those going. Dr. Talbert and family were soon placed on the going list, as he paid what he could and NASA picked up the tab for the rest. Having learned a lesson from the private corporation NASA then sent SCAMI a bill for the exact same amount for communication equipment, training and air time.

Resolved to make the best of migrating to Mars, Hanna wished to learn a useful vocation for herself. She would be seventeen when they left. Hanna being the daughter of two very intelligent professionals, was very smart, and capable. She was also very athletic. Desiring to remain athletic Hanna studied physical therapy. By the time they left to go to Florida for training she would have a certificate as a physical therapist.

When not involved with a launch or flight of a mission Dr. Talbert would be busy with his research. His passion was the asteroid belt. Raymond had been trying to map as many objects as possible. He had also been attempting to identify the makeup of each object. He was very certain that a wealth of minerals was available on these rocks. The difficultly would be living there while mining the asteroids. For this he had an idea that he needed to culminate further before voicing to anyone else.

Another of Dr. Talbert's assignments was to monitor the sun. Since the flare it had been determined that the Parker solar probe had continually accelerated with a sling shot effect around the sun then around Venus, over and over, getting closer and closer till the radiation had fried its circuitry and pulled it directly into the sun. With the incalculable speed the heavy matter had contacted anti matter within the sun and caused an explosion like never witness in history. This explosion had resulted in a solar flare and expulsion of solar particles which bombarded the system, and had zeroed in on the Earth.

During recent monitoring, the sun had returned to a normal state. In fact, regular spots and flares seemed to be minimized. Information collected during and since the flare was still being analyzed by experts around the world. New and amazing discoveries were soon to be revealed, not the least of which was antimatter. Its existence had been theorized for decades but now was a fact. Collecting or even how to handle it was as still a mystery.

The day arrived for the launch of Beta. She was to be the largest ship to attempt lift off from the planet. The plans for the next ship called for assembly in orbit. Beta would lift from Cap Kennedy in Florida. Nearly twice the size or the space shuttle it looked massive on the launch pad. The normal watch stations were pushed back by over half a mile. All air traffic was redirected east of the Mississippi river south of DC and north of the Yucatan. Millions of people from around the world was watching. Yes, the world was pretty much back to the way it had been.

The launch was picture perfect. SCAMI accepted the fact that the Public Relations benefit of so many viewers as a profit for the day. Already they had nearly filled the fifty seats for the next launch. They were even moving it up cutting the launch time in half. Another pilot and crew were being interview for the next flight, as Terry and Betty would be just leaving Mars when they intended to launch the next flight. Terry and Betty would just have to train for the flight after Gamma which was to be the next flight.

Beta upon its return would probably be a museum piece. Delta would be after Gamma, and when Gamma return it would be refurbished in orbit and readied for another trip out. A month after the launch of Beta, A1 would launch into orbit carrying components for orbital shipyard. There would be four such craft designed to obtain orbit with a payload and land back at the landing site in Florida. This would minimize the expense of building a shipyard and for bringing passenger to the transports.

The shipyards construction would be so that they could be used as a spaceport also. They would need to be able to not only build, and repair the transports Gamma and Delta, but handle fifty plus passengers being transferred from orbital craft to the transports. SCAMI was all in with the colonization of Mars. After the flare many with money were ready to leave Earth. With Gamma, and Delta being capable of multiple trips, and of carrying fifty passengers with personal items, the profit margin was getting better each trip.

Every ounce was paid for upfront by the colonist. Every candidate had figured the cost margin and had learned to go on a diet before weighing in for the trip. Every ounce they could lose was dollars in their pockets. More important to many was that weight off of their body resulted in more personal items they could take with them.

Dr Talbert and family didn't have to worry over this manipulation. They were considered priority colonist. Even so, before they arrived the first colonist voted the three of them into their elite status. This had even been confirmed with SCAMI. Dr. Talbert, Jessica, and Hanna were the only ones to ever receive such an honor. Later a city was named after Dr. Raymond Talbert, and a school after Hanna. Much before that though Dr. Talbert more than earned his recognition, but that too is for another story.

After overseeing the Beta launch and then the third launch of the orbital craft building Olympus the shipyard, Raymond and his family left for Florida. They would have a few months training then they would be transported to the Olympus yard. They would board Gamma for Mars just before Hanna's sixteenth birthday. Every piece of information on Dr. Talbert's research was on two micro drives. An original and a backup just in case. Over a thousand movies could be stored on one such drive. Each was nearly full with the data he had collected.

On Mars he would be much closer to the subject of his research. Therefore, he would have a greater opportunity to realize the completion of his dream. A comprehensive understanding of the makeup of the asteroid belt. Dr. Talbert was convinced of the importance of the belt to humanities future. In no way could he have imagined the effect the belt would have to mankind's destiny.

...

Across the world everything was very much returning to the way it had been before the flare. It had now been right at five years since the flare. All technology had been revived. The rollercoaster economy had begun to stabilize. On the farm north west of Dallas Bud had resumed a slow mundane life, with pleasure. He missed his granddaughters but was happy alone with his beloved wife.

A knock at the door startled them both early one evening. Answering the door Bud recognized the store owner he had made multiple delivers to during the disaster. The store owner wished to thank Bud for helping so many people during the bad times. He also gave Bud a very expensive bottle of wine. Bud told him he couldn't afford that expensive a bottle a wine, but the store owner told him it was a gift from all the people in the neighborhood which he had bought food to.

...

Craig and Melinda for the most part disappeared. On an irregular occasion they would show up in Dubois, but very rarely. They were very happy to live alone on top of their mountain with Jim. On the few occasions they appeared in town Gary would gladly meet them. To a large extent Gary admired them both. Many days he would look to the mountain and dream of the haven that the two of them shared.

...

Tom Backster had managed to survive the flare, and return completely to his digital existence. More or less enough said of a lonely man which only communicated with a cell phone or online. Who pushed people the same as numbers. A man who never knew the name of anyone he met, but knew the worth of every client to the penny.

...

Captain John Colson had a regular international route now. At least twice a week he would get to come home for a night or two. He was flying the best plane in the industry, with a great crew. His relationship with Jenifer was better each day they were together. Though he had many opportunities he had never cheated on Jenifer, and he was sure she had never cheated on him. That hadn't been their trouble in the past, they had just grown apart.

This time around he did his best to always show his love to Jenifer, and she showed respect to John in ways he needed most. Though there are always problems between any two individuals, with love and determinations they could and would flourish.

...

Jack had happily returned to retirement life. Fishing when he could, and keeping a small garden. Lately he was looking over the notes he had kept through the years thinking they would make a very interesting novel. One evening he opened a bottle of beer and started writing. Within a month he had what he thought would be an interesting story. To make sure he printed what he had and took it to his son that was an English teacher at the local high school, to proof read.

His son brought the book back a week later with few corrections saying he thought if would be worth publishing. With what any person goes through during a long life many interesting stories are available. Sometimes we just need to take notice. Often true life is stranger, and more fascinating than fiction.

Jason was back in the groove all the digital devices had been replaced and he was in his element. It had taken a couple of weeks for his muscles to quit aching from climbing poles and manually doing what now he could do with a push of a button. As he resumed his regular daily routine, he fondly remembered the task of the old ways.

...

Captain James Weaver and his submarine crew had returned to a normal schedule of patrolling the routes determined by the pentagon. X amount of days on patrol followed by X amount of days in harbor on leave. The flare had affected only slightly. It been a welcomed change of their routine.

...

At a meeting in the main habitat on Mars. Mark presented a finale proposal for laws governing the colony. They had each had a day to read and digest the contents. A motion to except was made and passed one hundred percent. Preparations to receive the next twenty colonists was discussed. The welfare of the two native born colonists was observed as was done each morning. They were each passed around for all to hold every morning.

Interconnected habitats had been completed, for sleeping quarters. Green houses were built and plants growing to provide food and oxygen. The colony was as ready as it could be for the new personnel. Emily was ready to give each a physical exam as they arrived and to handle the rash as they acquired it.

Beside the regular work which needed done they would have to start on new and larger habitats. As fast as they could. With another fifty settlers coming a little over a year and a half after this group, the facilities for them had to be completed. Fortunately, the plans for a city under a doom in the crater appeared to be very feasible. The first blocks had been fabricated out of the 3D printer, and proved to be perfect for the job.

The blocks were to be made to exacting specifications. When assembled as an igloo over the entire crater there would be three sets of steps going up the outside of the dome. They would fit so tight that the weight of those above would completely seal the dome. At two levels there would be a ledge wide enough to walk on the entire circumference. It would be a large undertaking to complete thus they would wait on the first reinforcements, to begin.

Janice White had designed, and drew up the plans for construction. Although they would wait for help to begin construction, they had started fabricating the building blocks. They had already built more atmospheric pressure pumps. Even more pumps would be needed. As White City which they had already named it was built, each section would be individually pressurized. This would protect the rest if one surface were to fail.

They had started expanding their survey area, searching for another location for a second city site. Not only would the cities need a protected location which could be sealed, but also needed natural resources. One item they could not fabricate and build was the 3D printer. A second was on the Beta ship on route to them. This new printer was an updated model capable of replicating parts to build another.

On board the Beta Terry and Betty were preparing to match orbits with the Mars lander. Upon matching orbits, they would detach a second lander that was attached to the underside of their craft. This lander was preloaded with supplies for the colony. Jacob, and Julia Wells would board it and pilot it down. They would also take Dan Freeman and Amy with them. After they started their descent, Terry attach the other lander to Beta, so the others settlers could board it.

The first colony was anxiously awaiting the arrival of lander 2. It was to land at a spot marked closest to the habitats. This was due to the load that it carried. Lander 1 with the bulk of personnel would land slightly further away. The people onboard would be in pressure suits, and could easily walk the distance. Jacob brought lander 2 down right on the mark set out for them. Shutting everything down they all exited the lander and went directly to the main habitat. There they all awaited the landing of lander 1.

Terry, and Betty had Beta in stable orbit and the lander was filled with settlers. They detached from Beta and began their descent. A guide beacon was pinging right in the center of the landing site. Just as Jacob had Terry brought lander 1 down for a perfect landing. By the time Terry had the lander shut down, the original colonist had formed a line between them and the main habitat. With smooth procession all of the settlers were guided inside.

Once inside a diagram of the loaded cargo on lander 2 was examined in preparation of unloading. Each article on board was marked as to what and where it should be placed. A human chain was formed and all hands pitch in together to unload the ship. A couple hours later everything had been unloaded. Jacob carried in his pocket a micro drive with private letters and photos for each of the original colonist. This was a welcomed surprise for them all. It was the first they had seen or heard from their families in over two years. Later that day they processed each of the new emigrants.

Breakfast was served at the exact time it always had been. Present was the entire colony, included their visitors Terry, and Betty. After a brief overview of the laws of the community assignments were made for loading out of lander 2. Terry would pilot lander 2 while lander 1 was left on site. The jewelry and a large amount of the red gold would be loaded for shipment to Earth. Since red gold wasn't available on Earth it was thought to be of great value. Also loaded was the new circuit boards they had made.

After the ship was loaded and all supplies had been put away the new settlers had time to acquaint themselves to their new home. The next day they would begin work on building White City. Janice White called a meeting with Amanda, Derrick, Randy, and Kevin. Janice showed them her ideas for White City and together they finalized the construction plan. She also showed them the building blocks they had made and where they had stored them near the crater.

Within a week construction had started on the city. Terry and Betty helped as needed as their launch date would be several months away. With the knowledge that Dr. Raymond Talbert would be arriving on the next ship the design plans were changed to include an observatory on top of the dome. An observatory without a large telescope, but with a very powerful digital camera remotely controlled. There would also be one placed lander 2 and left in orbit.

CHAPTER 9

Months had passed and the construction on White city was shaping up. The dome had been completed, and the entire city was pressurized. The interior was being worked up consistently. Those that farmed spent most of their time working on the crops. The jewelers split their time making jewelry to send to Earth, and working on the city. In this way they would certainly have the city ready before Gamma arrived.

The launch day was tomorrow, and the flight crew were preparing to leave. Letters and pictures were placed on a micro drive for Betty to carry back to the colonist's families. Terry, and Betty would take lander 2 up and reattach to Beta today. They would have to move everything going back to Earth before powering up Beta for the return trip. Lander 2 would then be left in orbit till needed by the Gamma crew.

Right on schedule the next day Beta left orbit with a burn towards the third planet, and home. Before blasting off Terry had checked the orbit of lander 2, and sent their goodbye's and well wishes to the Martian Colony. For the next two hundred and fifty days, Terry and Betty would be alone speeding in the direction of their home world.

At nearly the same time Gamma pushed away from the station Olympus. Gamma had a crew of four, and compliment of fifty paying settlers.

There were no first-class accommodations, in fact every seat was the same as the next. This said sitting in the very front row with a full inch more leg room sat Dr. Raymond Talbert and his family. This seat also assured that they would not have another reclined back in their laps during acceleration.

For 250 days they would be tied to these seats. Twice a day in rotation they would get up and walk back and forth front to back the entire length of the ship. Twice each day assigned personnel would get up and prepare a meal for everyone. As needed, there were facilities for and aft for them to use. There was no room nor little for them to do other than these coveted tasks. At roughly midpoint between Earth and Mars the two ships Gamma, and Beta were in constant communication. Though they would be near each there would be plenty of space between them. Traveling in opposite directions they would pass each other very rapidly.

Each day Dr. Talbert or one of the other trainers would stand at the front facing the others, and facilitate the lessons of pressure suit use or habitat construction. There were many lessons they had all heard before, but they were enthusiastic to discuss the conditions in which they would be living. The long trip was boring but restful, and they would all need that rest, as they would be extremely busy from the moment, on that they made orbit.

Finally, the Gamma approached Mars, and prepared to match orbits with lander 2. A pilot would go on board attach the lander with Gamma. Then they would disembark half of the passengers. Lander 2 would then detach and start its descent to the Mars Colony. Jacob would pilot lander 1 up to Gamma to unload the cargo for Earth which they had previously load on board. On reaching orbit, and attaching to Gamma they would unload, and then the other half of the settlers would board the lander. The Gamma crew too would land with the colonist, as they would have to wait a few months before launching back to Earth.

As each lander arrived on Mars they were met by the entire community. The doctor and her assistants screen each they were hustled into the meeting room which had been prepared. They had all been briefed on the rules and laws of the community, as well as having memorized a map of the facility. They had studied a design of White City but to see it in completion was still amazing.

...

Beta had been designed to launch and land on Earth. As they approached Earth, they made a low orbit then slowly descended towards the landing pad in Florida. All air traffic had been shut down for over two hundred mile in either direction. This precaution proved to be unnecessary as they sit down exactly on their landing site. The Beta ship would never fly again. It would become a museum piece though. Unloaded the cargo carried would bring very large profits for the stock holders of SCAMI.

As their profits grew so did the brazen arrogance of the SCAMI executives. Their communications to Mars was for more valuable cargo and more habitats for immigrants. The bottom line was profit. Quota's were being set for each trip. The corporation began threatening sanctions if these quotas weren't met.

Grumblings had begun to ramble through the colony. These rumors were hushed though as most weren't sure who to trust. It was well known that the original colonist had been corporate employed. The Gamma crew was still with them and they too were in the employment of the SCAMI corporation. Dissention was being felt through out the colony though.

...

By the time Gamma was to leave orbit for Earth, Dr. Talbert was eagerly viewing the asteroid belt. At this range the resolution was astonishing. He was learning much about the makeup of the belt. White City was completed with the exception of housing for the next fifty colonists. Even though some had complained about SCAMI at first everyone had settled into a daily routine. Work was progressing as it should. Exploration, and mapping was continuing on schedule.

A second location for a city had been found. It was a perfect location for an even larger city, but would require a substantial amount of labor. It was sixteen miles from base and just under fifteen miles from White City. Janice and the construction planning committee studied it for over a week before bringing a proposal before the congress. The congress was what the original colonist were now called. The plan was approved and soon work would begin. It would take over three years to complete.

Part of the design called for an eight-foot-deep, by ten-foot-wide trench to be dug between the two cities. Two four-foot diameter tubes would be place side by side and buried. Inside these tubes tightly fitting plug would be sent from one center to the other pushed by pressure. Inside each plug four people or a load of freight could be moved from one city to the other. One plug going either direction could be maintained.

Advancements and construction continued at an increasing pace on Mars. The second city was completed, and named Talbert. Talbert was almost twice the size of White with working space, living space and even had a school. Approximately ever year and a half, another load of fifty immigrants would arrive. Immigrates was a practical name now for they considered themselves an autonomous state.

SCAMI was putting more and more pressure on the leadership a Mars to increase profits. More and more ill feelings for the corporation festered amongst the colony. In a private meeting between the congress and governor, the entire original colonist, an idea was presented by Mark White. Mark suggested that they use the now large sums in their accounts on Earth to buy SCAMI stock. With a little luck and manipulating they just might be able to take over SCAMI.

Rebecca had been contacted secretly and begun discreetly buying out the stock. She had also been appointed legal representative for each of the original colonist. Before anyone was knowledgeable of what was happening, the Mars Congress owned seventy percent of SCAMI. Although profit would always be necessary for a successful corporation, it was no longer the driving force of this company.

Some of the later immigrates, seemed to be chosen more for there pocketbook than for their ability to or even desire to contribute to the colony. On arriving they seemed to think all they needed to do was lay around and pay to be waited on. In a big shock they learned that money was of no value on Mars. Some even seemed surprised to find out if they didn't work, they didn't get to eat.

The day they knew they owned control of SCAMI and the interests on Mars, they called for a meeting of all colonist. There was no room which could hold the entire colony now so many watched on closed circuit monitors. Mark addressed the Colony with the Congress holding hands behind him. "Today we have taken control of SCAMI and our own destiny. Today we say who will come to Mars and what they will pay. Today we say what and when we will send resources back to Earth. From today on we will govern Mars. Next week we will hold elections for governor of Mars, and for a third of the congress. Everyone over the age of eighteen will vote. In two days, you will submit candidates for each office. A legal candidate will need twenty signatures to be on the ballot. At any time, anyone has a problem that person should feel free to approach any representative, looking for an answer. One question will be on the ballot, do we at this time declare our Independence and send this declaration to Earth. Good day and God Bless you all."

Life on Mars was beginning to settle into a normal routine. Research, surveying, and mining were the main jobs. Also, of importance was climate control, energy, and construction. In one canyon the fine silicon power blowing through had formed fibers which hung from the overhangs almost like spiderwebs. At first sight the explorers thought they had found evidence of life. On farther examination it was determined that these strands were nature formations of silicon.

This silicon was collected for use in making clothing and making ropes. Later many other uses would be found for the fiber. The Mars Colony would prosper and grow. Man had now expanded to another planet.

...

The world had fully recuperated from the flare. Nathan was being promoted to Captain. The Dallas PD was an example for law enforcement around the planet. The County Electric Cooperative was on regular shifts now, and the power was flowing. Farmers were tending their crops. Craig and Melinda were raising their son Jim in a happy solitude. Gary got away for a couple weeks, and went up the mountain to visit his friends. In their happy and peaceful hideout Gary fished, and relaxed. Gary was amazed at the way little Jim had grown. So too had the Earth grown, for a time anyway people had become a little more caring, and helpful. As routines resumed so too did the arrogant attitudes of the average man.

Truly the world had returned to the ruts of its modern lifestyle.

THE END

If you enjoyed The Day The Earth Stopped give it
a positive review.

I have ideas for a following book, Mining the
Asteroids.

Also watch for To Run With The Big Dogs.

It is based on the life of my grandfather who
lived from 1889 to 1987

Made in the USA
Columbia, SC
14 December 2018